Seacliff
Chateau

Seacliff Chateau

✳ *Snowfall Wishes* ✳

JENNIFER GRIFFITH

Seacliff Chateau

ASIN: B09JHZ312C
ISBN: 9798751991630

This is a work of fiction. Names, characters, places, and events are creations of the author's imagination or are used fictitiously. Any resemblance to actual persons, living or dead, events, or locations, is purely coincidental.

Cover art credit: Blue Water Books

For Lorene, Amy, Beth, Kristie, and Emily

Whose Dad Ws a Skilled Woodworker

Chapter 1

Mallory

"I'm not a royalty stalker." I hid my phone in my pocket.

Emily snagged it out anyway. "Then what's this?" She pointed at my app, which was open. "Royalty Tracker USA?" A lifted brow accused me to my core. "This insanity has got to stop."

"It will. I promise." Well, it absolutely could after I'd met Prince Reynard—actual aristocracy—for whose newly purchased castle I was consulting on the renovation. Because Prince Reynard had to be my last chance at this coveted destiny. "Give me that." I took the phone back. "And give me a hug goodbye."

That's right. I did say castle. I was consulting on a castle renovation. *Buckworth Castle.* Cue my sigh of delight.

Emily and I embraced, and she patted my back. "I'm going to miss you! I can't believe we're spending the whole week of the holidays apart."

"First time ever. We won't even get to ice skate together." I sighed and pulled back to look at my cute former roommate. "But you have all your high-powered corporate deals going in Boston all season. It's not like you'd have time for me anyway."

Emily was impressive, no question. And too busy, especially this past year. She'd been highlighted as a rising star in the Boston money scene for her work at Pokoa Financial, the subject of numerous news articles, and she was dating her gorgeous coworker. How could I not be slightly envious? She was too nice and had been too generous with me for ages to let jealousy turn too green, of course.

"It doesn't mean I won't miss you. Can I come to Seacliff if I get a weekend?"

"Of course!" We hugged again, and I took my last bag out to my car. The clouds threatened, but no snow had fallen yet this year.

"Do you think we'll get the first snowfall soon?" She shaded her eyes and looked up at the weather. "If so, don't forget to wish on love."

I never forgot. And I always wished the same thing: that I'd meet and marry a prince—so that I'd never have to face poverty again.

Echoes of Scarlett O'Hara's determined cry—*"I'll never be hungry again!"*—filled my brain. Scarlett had the right idea.

It was probably childish to hold onto my adolescent wish, but in my heart, I secretly believed that locating and latching onto royalty was my number one best hedge against becoming destitute. Sure, I'd worked like crazy once I was old enough to get a job, and multiple jobs through high school and college, so there had usually been food in my cupboards.

However, I'd also chosen a career that my gut had told me would put me in the way of princes or dukes or barons.

And now it had! I was so close I could taste it.

"And don't you forget to wish, either." I waved and started my car.

"Of course!" She chased a little after me when I started rolling. "Oh, and if there are any hunky blue-collar types, send them my way."

There were always hunky construction workers, but I'd had my fill of them. Believe me. *Thanks a lot, Dylan.* "You can have them." All of them. It was weird how much Emily had a yen for them when she was entrenched in the white-collar world so deeply she couldn't see the sky.

"I like a guy who gets his hands dirty. Calluses are sexy. Although, yeah, a guy at work named Justin has asked me for drinks a few times,

2

so I might need to stop looking at construction workers."

Talk about downplaying her torrid romance with her coworker!

"You're one of a kind." I blew her a kiss goodbye and made my way to the interstate, singing to the radio. I headed through the tree-lined winding roads from Boston to Seacliff.

A few miles down the road, my phone rang, a call from my client—the one who was contracted with the prince.

I pulled over to answer. "Hi, Rochelle. I'm about an hour out. Anything new I need to know?"

"No, just checking your ETA. Your team should be arriving in an hour as well."

Team? I hadn't known there would be a team. "Good," I said anyway. I didn't like working with teams. On the other hand, maybe Prince Reynard was going to be on my team! "I am really excited to be working with Royal Construction." Even the name seemed to flash in neon that I was on track to reach my dream this time. Of course, it wasn't actual royalty, and I'd be working for Rochelle Kimball, not an actual queen, but I could still take it as a signpost for my journey toward my destiny, right?

"We feel lucky to have found you, Mallory. See you soon."

An hour later, I pulled up in front of the building at the address she'd given me.

What in the wide world?

I slowed way down, almost leery to approach. It might be catching.

Buckworth Castle was … lumpy.

Different styles protruded—like pimples on the façade of the house. A bay window here, a dormer there. Shutters? Check. Gothic arches? Check. Widow's walk? Of course! Why not? The thing was a hodge-podge mess from the exposed cracked foundation all the way up to the hexagonal cupola at the top.

Did I see hints of pink? Peeking through the peeling paint of missing slats of siding, pink stucco lurked.

Oh, brother. And don't get me started on the landscaping. It overhung the entire two-story box like a shroud. I bet the back aspect wasn't even viewable. I'd have to walk all the way around to see, but that much foliage generally only sprang up in swamplands or the Amazon.

Disaster.

It took all my willpower to get out of my car, it was that awful. No one had warned me! While I should have looked up Buckworth Castle online before coming, my policy was always to make my first impressions by experiencing a project in person, so as not to form any preconceived notions—for better or worse—based on tricks of photography.

Big mistake. If I'd known, even the inducement of a prince might not have been enough to get me here. Trust me: no one had gotten their buck-worth when they'd designed and decorated this monster.

With a series of steeling breaths, I tottered across the circular driveway toward the front door—which was intimidating, not just because it looked like it belonged in a historical horror movie, but because I was going to be tasked with doing something about it.

Me. Fixing this monstrous problem. Sure, I had a lot of experience with historical preservation, but this *thing* should not be preserved.

The owner probably did not want to hear that.

Worse, I was supposed to meet my *team.* Teeeeeeeam. A few minutes' reflection taught me there was no chance Prince Reynard would be on the team. Why should a team meddle in my work? Hadn't Rochelle hired me to be the authority on the subject? I did not need a team. I needed yes-men.

My skirt's hem caught on the bumper of a dilapidated work truck. It was like the thing wanted to hold me back, to save me from whatever horrors lay inside, but I forged on toward my fate.

However, Fate who brought me this pile-o'-tackiness also was leading me to the long-wished-for dream of meeting the prince, so I sucked up my courage, ousted my negativity, and determined to seize the day.

4

Chapter 2

Calder

Earlier the same day.

"What are you doing for the holidays, Mr. Kimball?" Maeve batted her eyelashes at me as she lingered at my classroom door. "Reading lots of history books?"

"Of course." That was a lie, no matter how much I wished it were true. "And you should, too."

"Oh, Mr. Kimball. You know we're going to be too busy skiing at San Moritz to do much reading."

"Naturally." Wealthy people. Far too busy for boring stuff like reading. "Well, don't eat all the candy from your Christmas stocking in one sitting, okay?"

She giggled. "Please. My parents aren't putting candy in my stocking this year—they're filling it with keys. I just got my license."

"Uh-huh." I picked up my jacket and the keys to my chambers. "Tell me what kind of car so I'll know what to watch out for." And avoid.

More giggling. "I'm a safe driver. And it's not a car, actually. It's going to be an SUV."

"Safer?"

"No, just posher."

The last thing that girl needed was more poshness. Neither she nor any of the students at St. Dominic's Preparatory Academy—feeder school for the Ivy League, third oldest in the New England area and with an excellent history curriculum—needed more luxury injected in their lives.

Even though I'd done everything I could over the past three years to avoid the ultra-wealthy, I couldn't exactly turn down the position of teaching Greek and Roman classics to motivated students in a small classroom setting. Plus, the campus was beyond beautiful with its architecture and serenity.

A history teacher's dream come true.

And that's all I ever aspired to be from now on, so it was perfect—despite my family's constant urgings to the contrary.

"Don't you have a train to catch, Maeve?" Dr. Shallenberger, the St. Dominic's principal, tapped Maeve on the shoulder and shuttled her aside.

"Bye, Mr. Kimball." Maeve batted her lashes again. "I won't forget you over the break. Don't forget me." She waved, fingers only, and left.

"Oh, brother," Dr. S. said as soon as Maeve was out of earshot. She smoothed her dress. "It's the seventeen-year-olds you have to watch out for."

"Right." And the forty-seven-year-olds, too, if Dr. Shallenberger's frequent attentions were a clue. "Trust me, my guard is up." Against all of them.

"Family plans for the holidays? Or a vacation, like you really deserve?" She leaned against the doorframe in exactly the same way Maeve had. "Relaxing on some tropical sands? Or are you heading to that Wildwood Lodge in upstate New York again this year for extensive reading?"

"I wish." That reminded me. I picked up a few books to take with me. My parents couldn't need me to work eighteen-hour days, right? There would be time to dig into this new analysis of the life of

6

Alexander the Great. Surely. "I'm heading to an island, but not that kind. Somewhere much colder and definitely not tropical: Rhode Island."

"Oh, I have a sorority sister on the coast in a small town there. She's living in her husband's great-grandparents' grand estate. He's is a mover and shaker in Seacliff. Very swanky."

Again with the wealth references. "It's not for a vacation. I'll be working."

"Your parents' business suck you in again?" Dr. Shallenberger knew my secret identity, but with any luck, she'd been keeping it to herself.

"Afraid so." *Very afraid.* "But I should be able to get in and out quickly and be done by the new year."

"With time to read." She swiveled a little. "Or visit friends."

Friends. All my friends had married or moved out West. Books were my friends.

"I mean," she drew a circle on the hardwoods with her shoe's tip, "I've got a place in Manhattan for the break. If you want to celebrate New Year's Eve and watch the apple drop, I'd welcome the company."

Oh. So that's what she was saying. "Thanks."

I clammed up. She was crossing a line, and she'd recognize it later when she replayed our conversation in her mind. No sense highlighting how inappropriate it was—even for private-school administration.

"Bye." I locked my door and left her in the hallway.

My old truck was already packed, so I just dropped off a few things in my chambers and then got on the road. No sense prolonging the inevitable.

The ninety minutes sped by as I listened to my favorite history podcast, this week's show an in-depth look at the emperor Nero—villain or the victim of bad press? Soon, I was pulling up in front of—uh-oh.

My neck pulled backward. It was all I could do not to put the truck in reverse. What in the world had Mom and Dad taken on as a project?

If all the periods of architecture in the history of the world—from cave-dwelling to 1960s post-modern could have been combined into one amalgamated lump—it would be Buckworth Castle.

"Calder! You're here!" Mom appeared, jogging toward me from the menacing heap of stones that someone had decided to arrange as a dwelling. "How do you like Buckworth Castle?"

"I hate it." Why lie?

"You're just being negative." She hugged me and hooked her arm through mine. "Oh, all right. Fine. It's the worst thing I've ever seen in my life, too." Mom had seen some bad heaps of lumber and sheetrock in her day, so that was saying something.

"I think they gave it a couple of facelifts over the years. But more in the vein of covering up, rather than making the most of what was there."

I pictured Buckworth as the equivalent of an aging movie actress whose lips were stretched to look like Batman's nemesis the Joker—no longer recognizable after too many plastic surgeries.

"Look past the cosmetic and see the good. The cupola. That's good." My mom, the relentless optimist. "Plus, if we can get some of the landscaping debris cleared out around the ocean side of the house, it might open up the view as well as give us a clue as to its original glory."

I may have choked on her use of the word glory. I patted my throat. "That many trees could fuel a hundred homes for three winters."

That said, the ocean was audible—crashing in regular, soothing rhythm. And Mom might be right about the view. There was supposedly a cliff back there. I strained to see it, but it was no use.

"Don't bother with your bags and things yet. We've got project headquarters in the pool house out back, and you'll be staying in one of the cottages along the cliff, but for now, let me give you the grand tour. Or, the not-so-grand tour, as the case may be."

"Why did you say yes to this job? And couldn't you have convinced the owner to demolish and start over?"

"One does not simply tell Prince Reynard what to do." Mom gave a weird nod of her head like she was pretending to be a movie character bowing to a regent.

"*Prince* Reynard? Is he actually a prince? As in actual royalty? Or more one of those, ah … hip-hop princes, like a prince fresh out of Bel Air?"

She busted a hip-hop dance move for four counts. "European. We probably shouldn't have said yes to the job, but Dad and I decided this Christmas we were giving ourselves the gift of *a challenge!*" She shook her free fist in the air.

"Challenge." Great. "And so this challenge is my holiday gift too, I take it?"

"No. For you, the gift is *family togetherness.*" She pecked my cheek and opened the creaking wooden door into the dim of the house.

A large room, with walls of almost cobblestone, reminded me of a Hollywood movie set from the 1930s when they were trying to portray a medieval castle. An open stairway stretched up the curve of the far wall. An enormous fireplace with a rough-timber mantel gaped its soot-filled maw at us.

Yet, above us hung mid-century modern light fixtures. Steel and glass with geometric design. Then, the doorways were Mission style, curved with heavy barn-wood doors and long wrought-iron hinges with arrows on the ends. Naturally! Ugh.

The style mash-up went on and on. Everything—from the Victorian wall hangings to the African safari skin rugs on the floor—was a colossal mess.

"When was this built?" From my study notes, most of the great seaside mansions on this part of the Atlantic coast were constructed during the Gilded Age by the captains of industry of the 1890s as retreats from the city. "I feel like I'm standing in time's blender." And getting seasick.

"Not sure, but from the avocado green appliances and general lack of taste, should we guess nineteen seventies?"

I doubted it, but whenever it was built or remodeled, nothing made sense in the design or the decorating. "And you and Dad are supposed to do ... what with it?"

"Restore it."

But there was nothing to restore it to. "To what it was originally, or to what it should have been, if the builders had had brains in their heads?"

"We're still negotiating that point with the client."

"The prince." Probably some low-grade wannabe aristocrat from Europe calling himself a prince to get attention. Most royal families had melted away in the past few decades, leaving just wealthy families instead—or not-so-wealthy families with vestigial titles. It had started with the 1832 Reform Act in England, and ended in the destruction of hundreds of country house estates. ... But I digress.

"He has his own ideas. To help, we've hired Ms. Jameson, a consultant who specializes in historic preservation. You'll be working hand-in-glove with her to get things exactly right."

Great. Just great. Exactly what I needed, some snooty old woman who thought she knew everything about historical importance to micromanage my work. Could this job get any worse? Apparently it just had, thanks to the looming judgmental eye of Ms. Jameson peering over my shoulder all day. I pictured a statue of Medusa, with all her snake-hair afloat, ready to turn me to stone.

"Well, I want to get started as soon as possible." Or, I should say, *get it over with*. "But, let me register my opinion that the best plan of action for this lump-of-coal-that-will-never-become-a-diamond is this: total demolition."

A horrified gasp in female tones sounded behind me.

Mom raced to her side. "Ms. Jameson! I'm so pleased you're here."

I turned to see not a lethal Medusa but a brunette, nubile *Venus*.

Chapter 3

Mallory

The front door was ajar, and I stepped inside. Voices came from a few paces away, and I crossed the stone floor into a vast, high-ceilinged room with rock walls and—

"—the best plan of action for this lump-of-coal-that-will-never-become-a-diamond is *total demolition*."

I gasped. "No!" squeaked out of me. If they demolished Buckworth Castle, then my role also evaporated. And I hadn't even met Prince Reynard yet. "You can't do that."

"Ms. Jameson! I'm so pleased you're here." A tall, warm-countenanced woman rushed toward me with arms open. "You made it. I'm Rochelle." My new boss warmly welcomed me, pulling me toward the young man who'd made the *let's tear down this house* comment. She introduced me to him. "This is Ms. Jameson."

Whoa. Who was he? Young, gorgeous, and built like a demi-god of Greek proportion. Dark hair, narrow but strong nose, piercing dark gaze. Could this be my long-awaited moment? Was *he* Prince Reynard?

He looked taller in person than in his photos, and much more fit. More rugged. However, in the online pictures he'd also turned his head aside and avoided paparazzi so notoriously that this was my first real look at him.

And what a look it was.

No wonder he wanted to stay out of the spotlight. With his wealth and status *on top of* those looks, he'd be swarmed by gold-diggers everywhere he went.

What was proper? Maybe we peasants weren't supposed to meet their eyes. But his eyes were dragging me in, like an anchor's chain being slowly cranked upward. I was caught in his dark gaze.

Just to be safe, I crossed one foot behind the other, bent my knees and bowed my head. A perfect curtsey. I looked up, and Rochelle's eyes were dancing. The prince's were cold.

"Ms. Jameson, this is your team member, Calderrrr—"

"Calder Kimball," he interjected. "Nice to meet you. I guess I'm your team."

My team. Calder the Neanderthal construction worker. *Not the prince.*

Annnnd, I'd curtseyed to him. If only the floor could swallow me now. Instead, I had to feign manners.

"Nice to meet you," I managed, stepping closer so I could see him in the light. Now that he wasn't the prince, he looked scruffy and tired. A construction worker like Dylan and the others, through and through. I sobered and cleared my throat. "What will your role in the project be?" I may as well ask up front. Then I could assert my authority—right from the get-go. "Since I'll be making the historic preservation decisions."

He glanced at Rochelle. "Craftsman. As usual." He had a different drawl to his voice than I'd expected. Not at all back-country. More like highbrow Boston or Baltimore. And there was something in his eye … something like high intelligence. "Unless there's more I haven't heard yet?"

Rochelle placed an arm around his shoulders and gave a quick squeeze. "Master craftsman. And you'll take all your cues from Ms. Jameson."

12

"Call me Mallory." I took his proffered hand, and whoa. Something jarred in me. Also not what I'd expected—nor something I could define. The calluses on the side of his thumb were rough, manly, and ...

I jerked my hand back down by my side. No construction worker or craftsman would be creating jarrings up my arm. Not when a prince was basically standing at my threshold.

"Since we won't be tearing down and starting over, what is the plan?" I turned to Rochelle. She was the project boss. "Does Prince Reynard have specifics?"

"We're still negotiating that, but I'm encouraging him to pinpoint a single time period for his restoration plan." Rochelle led me through the oversized room and into the kitchen—which had been decorated by what must have been a cloister of circus refugees. Everything came in wide red and white stripes, from the tile floor to the wallpaper to the stove hood. "As you can see, there is a lot of work needed."

A lot! More like a whole subdivision worth of work. "You initially gave me a six-week timeline."

"That was before we were aware of the extent."

"Hey." Beside me, Calder the Craftsman grumbled. "Six weeks is all you get."

Rochelle shot him a look then returned a steady gaze to me. "Six weeks is still going to have to be our goal, I'm afraid."

Calder muttered something that sounded less offended and then said aloud, "Can we shorten that?"

Ha! As if! "This is more like a six-month project. Maybe a six-year project, if you ask me." I might have been out of line, but ... well, maybe stretching it longer would end up being in my best interest. "I'll stay as long as you need me, Rochelle."

"That's sweet, but we should be able to finish in that timeframe. That's what we do at Royal Construction and why we get hired by elite clients."

There was a scoffing sound from Calder's direction. He really

13

shouldn't scoff at his boss. What was his deal, anyway?

In walked someone else, a middle-aged man with the same strong, narrow nose I'd seen on Calder. Those seemed to be going around.

"Hey, honey." Rochelle gave a man a side hug. "This is Mallory Jameson. I've been telling you about her."

"Our historic preservation consultant. Good. You come highly recommended." He shook my hand. "I'm Darren, Rochelle's worse half. I have word from Prince Reynard that he'll be with us for dinner tonight to make some decisions. We'll want both of you there." He indicated Calder and me.

"Dinner? Tonight?" My throat squeezed to the diameter of a juice-box straw, and my voice showed it. "With the client?"

With the prince!

I should not squeal. Neither now nor when I was introduced to him. And I probably shouldn't curtsey, either, if recent moments had taught me anything.

"How does one dress for dinner with royalty?"

"To quote Jane Austen," Calder chuckled, "Just wear whatever you have that's best."

"Right," Rochelle said. "In fact, dinner should be ready soon. Fifteen minutes?" She and Darren left the room.

Craftsman Calder must have noted my shock. "Maybe you don't like anyone quoting Austen. You're looking pale."

"I'm not pale." I was probably pale. Since when did construction workers … never mind. "And I'm not going to be one of those girls who wears an evening gown to a business meeting." Yes, I'd packed an evening gown. I'd found it with Emily at a second-hand shop when I visited her in Boston. No, I wasn't wearing it tonight. "That's embarrassing."

Rochelle popped her head back in to give me lodging instructions and a key. "I'll see you at dinner, Mallory."

Calder looked over his shoulder at me as he left, too, and I headed to my cottage to unpack.

There, I shot a quick text to Emily. *It's already happening. I'm meeting the prince!*

Are any other guys there? Does the prince have a friend?

The only other single guy so far is a construction worker. To whom I'd bowed like he was the fabulously wealthy son of aristocrats. And I had to see him again tonight. At dinner. And he was distractingly handsome. *No! I would not be distracted.*

And? Is he cute? Would I like him?

Every single job I'd been on had been rife with amorous construction workers—who refused to take no for an answer. Like Gardner. And Dylan.

My skin crawled. Stupid Dylan.

I'm stuck as a two-man team with the construction guy, and he's coming to dinner with me and the prince.

Chapter 4

Calder

Even though their hired chef had everything under control in the kitchen, Mom and Dad insisted that our family help out with the meal. I was tasked with setting the table—the exactitude of which had never been my forte.

"Aren't these going to be our best holidays ever?" Mom placed ice cubes in the goblets with tongs. "This job is a physical and mental and historical challenge, and we're together. These holidays are going to be perfect."

Well, not perfect, maybe, but they weren't going to be the worst. The worst holidays had already occurred. Luckily, I'd figured out how to guarantee nothing like that awful year would ever repeat.

"I must say, Mom, you have an unusual view of what constitutes the perfect Christmas." Work, work, work. Work until you drop. Which was why last year I'd fled the Royal Construction holiday scene and tried to hole up in Wildwood Lodge.

That … had only distracted me temporarily.

"Togetherness is the perfection." Mom sighed and paused, staring at me with that too-familiar look. "Dad and I have each other. Not to bring up the obvious, but when are you going to try to win back Alanis?"

Never? "We've both moved on."

"Not from what I hear about her—or what I see in you. Come on, Calder. She was your ideal match."

On paper. Yeah, she had been. But that paper, and her façade, had all been paper-thin. "Alanis isn't on my radar." Unless as a red-blinking blip of an enemy battleship.

"Whatever did you do to lose her?" Mom finished with the clink-clink of ice into glass and moved to pouring water. "You never explained. If you would, maybe I could suggest a way to get her back. For one, you didn't go after her when she left."

No, I hadn't. Especially since I'd been the one who'd kicked her and her conniving family to the curb, only staying out of a lawsuit against them for fraud by their concession of signing a gag order. "You're right. I didn't elaborate on our breakup, and no, I didn't try hard enough, Mom."

"But you're alone—and at your age."

"I'm practically Methuselah." Thirty-two was close to ancient, at least to Mom, who'd married at nineteen. "Don't worry about me. I have my books."

"Books!" Mom dropped the ice tongs into the metal bowl with a clank. "Books can't keep you warm at night."

Dad sauntered in with a cutting board of fresh, hot bread. "They can if you burn them." His chortle filled the whole pool house, echoing off the indoor pool's surface. "Let him be, Rochelle. We can trust he will find the right woman at the right time."

"Thanks, Dad." Since there were zero right women, that was probably true. I could concede that point to him.

"If you'd just let a woman or two know who you are, that you're heir of our family's entire business—"

I cleared my throat so loudly that its echo bounced between the tile ceiling and floor. "Mom."

"Oh, fine."

If it was up to me, no one would know my name had ever been Calder *Royal* Kimball. I'd even dropped the middle name legally last year, turned it into a plain old R. It was so much easier that way. I could just be myself, read my books, teach my lectures, and have nothing to do with Royal Construction.

Well, except at holidays.

I might not be the ideal heir for Mom's grandparents' construction dynasty, but I also wasn't a cruel, family-rejecting son. Mom and Dad were excellent people. Alanis O'Houlihan and her ilk were not Mom and Dad's fault. In fact, they had no idea about her crimes against humanity—er, against this human—and I planned to keep it that way.

"Here are the place cards." Mom set them all out.

Aw, no! "You can't put me next to that Mallory person." No matter how gorgeous her shiny dark hair was, swinging in a long ponytail. Or those curves on her petite frame. Or those dark eyes. She'd curtseyed to me, for heaven's sake! At that, my hackles had gone up, big time—worried she'd done her research, dug into who I was. No matter how hard I tried to bury my identity, the resourceful ones had their ways to find out who I was. "I'll work with her, but don't even think about matchmaking."

"Me?" Mom touched her collarbone. "I'd never!" A smile tugged at the side of her mouth, making me drag out a sigh. "It's more about collaboration. You and Mallory are the only two people educated enough on the topic to please the prince. But together you can guide him toward … tastefulness."

I wasn't letting that dark-eyed woman get her hooks into me. "Where did you find this Mallory person?" That was the big question: whether Mallory had sought out Mom or vice versa.

"Stop calling her *that Mallory person*. She came highly recommended on a morning television program I was watching. We were really lucky to get her. She's more of an expert than she might look at first glance. She was in charge of the Delancy mansion

18

renovation in the Hamptons, another historic mansion on Long Island, and was even involved in a reworking of something not far from here in Newport. Don't alienate her with your cold stares, please. We need her. In fact, *you* need her. Without her, this job will take much longer than six weeks."

Perish the thought. "I have a classroom. A commitment to the students. They're counting on my return." Several people had said so explicitly, including Dr. Shallenberger *and* Maeve.

"It's not where your real talent lies, son. It's not your destiny."

Destiny. Pah. "Six weeks is all I can give here in Seacliff without breaking a contract." Contracts were everything to Mom and Dad's business. That got her, finally.

"Okay, keep your contract's terms. Six weeks here. Fine." She wagged a finger at me. "But this is exactly why I want you to work closely with Mallory Jameson. Get it?"

"Fine." But I wasn't sitting by her at dinner, no matter what her qualifications. I swapped the cards and placed her a few people away.

Mom swapped them right back. "I can't have her seated next to Prince Reynard." She shot me a look, like I should have seen this fact.

So, Mom would rather have Mallory try to dig my gold than the prince's.

Anyway, I was definitely in shields-up-mode enough that I could fend off the attacks of weird girls who bowed to me as if *I* was the royalty. Weird girls were not my thing, never had been.

Yeah, my thing had been two-faced women like Alanis O'Houlihan who told me every lie I ever wanted to hear.

Speak of the weirdness, in walked Mallory. Her long, dark waves of hair spilled over her shoulders, catching the light from the table's candles with a glistening. She'd applied makeup? If so, it'd been understated and done with an expert hand—unlike any of the teenagers I dealt with all day. Just enough to enhance what she had. And wow, she had a lot. Huge, dark eyes, like a baby deer's. Long lashes all around them, which fell and raised slowly, captivating me. And as she removed her parka, she revealed a petite yet curvaceous figure. I couldn't stop looking at the curve of her waist, how it …

No. Nope! I was not looking.

Nor was she looking at me. In fact, as she met my gaze, she quickly averted her eyes and whirled around to face the wall.

Well. That was new. Usually women let their stares crawl all over me. Fine. Maybe it was all right that she sit next to me. She might smell nice if she looked that good. I hoped she'd ignore me this well all throughout dinner, zero conversation, with the possible exception of work topics.

That'd be great by me.

She passed me, though, on her way to hang up her parka, and I caught the faintest scent of some kind of heavenly jasmine. I let my eyes drift shut and remembered a garden I'd walked through in Italy, where jasmine climbed the old stone wall.

"Hallo, good evening." A clatter at the door, and the prince came in. I'd never met him, but he was unmistakable. Prince Reynard's hair was a few inches too long, he was a few years older than me, and a couple inches shorter than me—and I'm no NBA basketball candidate. However, to make up for it, he wore a crisp suit and starched shirt, complete with shiny cuff links. His shoes shone enough I could've used them as a mirror for shaving.

Which—uh, I should've shaved this week.

Finals. There hadn't been time.

Prince Reynard made me feel like a slouch.

For a few minutes, after Mom made introductions, we discussed business matters regarding the so-called castle.

"It is my belief we should create the world's most unique home, right here at Buckworth Castle." Prince Reynard had one of those French-German-Italian accents I couldn't pinpoint. "The best. The finest. And did I mention, most unique?"

Mission accomplished already. Because unique was the only polite word any of us could apply to it.

"Do you have an era you'd like to pinpoint, Your Grace?" Mom winced as if she weren't sure whether *Your Grace* was the right thing to apply. We Americans don't go in for titles. In fact, they're explicitly banned by the Constitution.

Article one, section nine. The foreign emoluments clause.

I'd mention it to Mom *after* we'd convinced His Majesty to tear down this house.

"Buckworth has a lot of potential." Mallory gave a little half-laugh. "But right now, it's a terror."

No one else breathed. Mom met my gaze, then Dad's.

Mallory, however, blundered on. "Mentally, I'm calling that kitchen area the Big Top."

"Big Top?" Reynard frowned while the rest of us tried hard not to visibly cringe. "As in, P.T. Barnum designed it? Yes, I can see that." He chortled—and we let out our collective breath.

Who did Mallory think she was? She could really mess things up with the client. I tried to catch her eye and warn her to shut it down, but she studiously avoided looking at me.

Which was simultaneously refreshing and frustrating.

Girls were usually annoyingly into me. I guess I'd taken that for granted.

We sat down, and the chef served our dinner—bringing the prince's plate first.

Prince Reynard merely picked at his sweet potato hash with ham and pecans. Mistake—since it was really good. Wildly better than anything I got in my chambers at St. Dominic's, even though they boasted as having the best chefs in all private-schooldom.

If you asked me, those St. Dominic's chefs were the leftovers after Mom and Dad had hired the best.

Apparently, that Mallory person beside me agreed.

"This is so good." Mallory lifted forkful after forkful into her mouth, barely taking time to chew in between. "Is there more?"

Mom asked the chef to bring another helping for Mallory.

21

As she ate, Mallory closed her eyes, savoring each bite. She chewed and swallowed and smiled and emoted with joy every time she tasted a new dish. "I thought the hash was good, but have you tried the fruit compote? Mmm!"

Our royal guest watched her with what looked like amusement. Soon, he said what we were all thinking. "Miss Jameson eats deliciously." Then, he took a larger bite of his own. "She makes me enjoy my own food even more." He chewed and swallowed, and then ate another. "Yes, indeed. Much more." His eye twinkled at her.

Huh.

Did I mention she was weird? I should've said really weird. As weird as the dancing plague of St. Vitus in the Middle Ages.

The prince's phone rang, and he excused himself and went outside. Once he was gone, I grabbed Mallory's arm below the table.

"What are you thinking?"

"I'm not thinking. I'm eating." She took another bite, letting out a huge sigh.

It was sexy, and it captured me for a moment. The way she ate was something from a late-night naughty movie, but luckily I caught my thoughts quickly. "I meant, what are you doing telling Prince Reynard his kitchen looks like it was attacked by circus clowns?"

"I'm doing us all a favor." She took two more bites and chewed them, her jaw's line drawing my eye against my will. "This food is so good, by the way. It's amazing."

"Well, you're eating it like a crazy person." Like she'd been starved half her life. Her curves told a different story. "What's with all the dramatics?"

"Apparently you don't have a true appreciation for food."

"Ugh, you're not a foodie, are you? Please." People whose whole lives revolved around their next plate of food drove me insane. It was always *goat cheese this* and *organic hummus that*.

She set down her fork and leveled a look at me that could have turned me to stone. *Ah, as predicted, Medusa has appeared.* "Don't act

22

like you know anything about me."

A lump of something clunked into my gut. It might have been humility.

"I'm so glad the two of you are getting along, really hitting it off." Mom beamed at me and Mallory—a warning beam. "Since you'll be working together nonstop, it's a good thing you're making friends."

"Friends here for sure." Mallory smirked at me out of Mom's view. "Bosom buddies."

Her phrase, naturally, made my eye dart to her bosom and back to her eye.

I was not thinking about her full bosom or about the bold and unusual woman herself or what she might have meant by that *don't act like you know me* comment.

Her assertion did not feel like a challenge. At all.

Chapter 5

Mallory

"It's a good thing you're making friends." Rochelle beamed at me like I was a school project she'd gotten an A on. "Go on, you and Calder get to know each other. Darren and I are heading inside to do the dishes, so you two just relax. Set a fire, if you like."

"A pool house with a fireplace, and an indoor pool. This is what I'm talking about. Thanks." However, I didn't sit tight like she'd asked. Instead, I took my dishes and some others to the kitchen. Calder followed me—unfortunately. Despite an intense scan of the area between the pool house and the cooking cottage, I couldn't lay eyes on Prince Reynard. And Calder was dogging my steps.

Bummer. Where had Reynard gone? We'd just been getting our chemistry going! When I first saw him, I hadn't been blown away by his looks. More like, *huh. Not bad.* Mainly, it had been because he could use a haircut, but on the plus side, he dressed like a magazine model, and he had some serious charisma going on. The way he carried himself, his sheer confidence—it was undeniably attractive. Plus, he had a good smile and a friendly demeanor I hadn't expected. In fact, he seemed almost down-to-earth. The more I got to know him, the more

I'd see his personal charms, for sure. "Prince?" I asked into the night.

No reply.

"What are you looking for?" Calder said. "Did you drop something?"

If Calder hadn't been lurking near my shoulder, I would've texted Emily to tell her that Prince Reynard found my food enthusiasm charming.

Unlike Calder. Who'd called it ridiculous.

"My plans." Smirk. *To chase down Prince Reynard and go on a moonlight walk with him.*

"You two go on, now." Rochelle shuttled us back toward the pool house.

"Fine, since we're being coerced, go ahead. Tell me about yourself." Calder walked beside me, but instead of going in, he took me past the row of cottages, down a little path lined with manicured Italian cypress trees jutting skyward. "Ten fast facts."

"What's that?"

"Just what it sounds like. Speed-small-talk." He crunched along the narrow gravel path, his shoulder bumping mine once or twice. "Let's get it over with."

"Wow, am I that fascinating?" Sarcasm wasn't usually my thing, but he was being pretty rude. "How about you start? I don't have ten facts about myself on the tip of my tongue."

"Sure, you don't."

A cold breeze blew. Either it was from the nearby ocean or it was from Calder. What was his problem? Geez.

"Fine." I could probably muster something. "I'm from Albany, but I prefer small towns, even though I live in the city now. I have a few distant cousins but no siblings." I left out a lot there about my family, but he didn't need to know any of that. Just like he didn't need to know why I felt compelled to eat when there was food. "In college I realized I was fascinated by history and architecture and tried to figure out how to combine them into a career, so I landed in historic preservation consultation. My hobbies, if I ever get to them, are reading ridiculously long history books—I totally geek out over them—going for long drives and stopping at every historical marker, and someday I dream of going to Europe, especially southern Europe to see Rome and Greece, to study the ancient architecture and see the museums."

Calder stopped me in my tracks, a murderous look in his eye. He searched—deeply—scanning, penetrating like a javelin into my brain through my eye socket.

Finally, I couldn't take it. I blinked and turned away. "What's with you?" I pulled my coat tighter around my body, since his piercing gaze had made me feel naked. "Stop being like that." I stepped back from him. An owl hooted in the distance, and the salt of the sea put a tang in the air.

"Where did you come up with that story?" His jaw clenched and pulsed. "Who did you talk to?"

Now who was the one being ridiculous? "I'm sorry, but you're not very good at light small talk. Has anyone ever told you that?"

"Neither are you." He frowned even more deeply.

I stepped around him and continued on the path. Somewhere nearby, waves crashed in regular rhythm. "I'm going to see the waves." Maybe they'd rinse off whatever toxin Calder Kimball was pouring on me. "Excuse me." I practically marched down the path, labyrinthine though it was.

Ooh, and maybe Reynard had gone on a night walk, too. I could meet him by the sea. So romantic—if third-wheel Calder ever got the hint.

A cloud floated over the moon, and I had to pull out my phone to use as a flashlight. A second later, the light doubled, and there was Calder adding his flashlight to mine, keeping pace with me.

"What was your major?" he demanded.

"History." I was clipped and terse. "Emphasis on Western European history, post Renaissance. My senior thesis was on historical architecture in New England."

26

"Oh." This seemed to disappoint him. "But you said you wanted to see Greece and Rome."

"Who wouldn't?" I walked a little faster. Maybe Prince Reynard had wandered down this path to view the ocean, as well. I'd like to run into him. And if there was a cliff, bonus! I could push Calder off it.

Okay, I wouldn't, but he was definitely asking for some kind of violent reaction.

"Where did you go to school?" More grilling.

"Just a small community college first, and then I got into SUNY at Albany. I needed to live at home."

"Oh." This, too, seemed to come as a blow. He practically hissed with the deflation of whatever had puffed him up a few minutes ago. "Not Ivy League?"

"Are you questioning my credentials?" I stopped, and he bumped into me hard. "Because I assure you, despite my so-called inferior education at a less prestigious institution, I have a firm grasp on historical details of all eras in question for Prince Reynard's project. I have strong experience and even stronger references. I did my practicum at the New York State Historical Society in their architectural archives. You don't need to be a jerk about it. Just ... go back to the house or whatever. I don't really care about hearing your ten speed-dating facts or whatever. I think I already know all I need to know about you and your snobbish deal."

He was a carpenter. Who was he to judge my education?

Frustrated, and with no prince in sight, I hustled back to my cottage that was nestled in the copse of trees behind the awful castle. I slammed the door. I would not see the ocean that night. Waves crashed angrily on the rocks. Or maybe that was the blood rushing in my ears.

Calder Kimball was officially off my people-I-talk-to-casually list. Worse, he'd made me miss the chance to run into Prince Reynard by happenstance at the ocean.

Working with Calder was going to be the hardest part of the hardest job I'd ever been hired to do.

A soft knock came on my door.

The prince? My heart pounded. I paced myself going to answer it. "Hello?"

It wasn't the prince. Sad. But happily, it wasn't Calder, either.

"Hi, Mallory." Rochelle smiled at me, passing me an additional blanket—the fuzzy kind with a fleece lining. Mmm. "Calder said you two went for a walk to the ocean. How nice."

Not that nice, actually. I pulled a wan smile.

Rochelle returned it.

"Is something wrong?"

"No, no. Not at all. Prince Reynard has made a decision, and I'm here to let you know that you'll need to research Georgian woodworking."

"Georgian!" But that was the sole era not represented in the architecture of the place.

Rochelle closed her eyes for a moment as if gathering strength. "Yes, and it will be perfect when we're finished. Because that's what Royal Construction does: perfection."

"Perfection." From this heap. Wow. Rochelle's bosses at the construction firm she contracted for were asking for miracles. Why they'd bid on this job mystified me. "It's a big ask, you know." Maybe I should forget it. Awkwardly give Prince Reynard my number and leave.

Rochelle gave me one of those *I know what you're thinking* looks. "Perfection comes at a price. Now that we've seen the scope of work, you'll be paid a bonus." She named a large number.

Well, that was a hefty inducement. Some of that money could go in my bank account. With the rest, I could buy a year's supply of food, just to keep on hand—and it wouldn't all have to be canned green beans and macaroni and cheese, either.

Reluctantly, I nodded assent.

"So we're on." She gave a loud clap and grinned. "That's great. Now, you'll design all woodworking for the interior, and Calder will bring it all to life. Prince Reynard has selected woodwork as his highest priority. He wants 'every wall clad in wood.'" Rochelle made air quotes.

"Every wall?" The place had to be ten thousand square feet. With towering walls. "That's ... a lot of wood."

"He prefers mahogany."

That was a *lot* of mahogany. "I'm on it."

"I've already let Calder know. He is anxious to get started first thing in the morning. Perhaps you've heard he is on a tight timeline."

What, he had a construction workers bar to get down to? Yeah, he could meet up with Dylan and his buddies and swap stories about their lack of success hitting on me. "Oh?" I managed politeness.

"Yes, despite his magnificent, one-of-a-kind skills, he's got a job in the wrong profession elsewhere."

Um, what? "He's not a full-time carpenter?"

"No." She frowned and rolled her eyes. "For now, he's a history teacher at a private Ivy League prep school near Boston, and his break is only so long." Rochelle sighed like this choice was her life's biggest disappointment. "He only agreed to come work during the break because Darren and I leaned on him. For that reason, and others—like meeting timelines, as the company is famous for doing—we don't want to drag this out. You understand."

I did not understand. Not one bit, but I nodded and went back inside.

Calder Kimball wasn't a construction worker? He was a history teacher at an Ivy League prep school?

I sat down hard on the bed. For a second, I picked up my phone to text Emily the curious facts, but I wasn't even sure how to word them.

Instead, I got to work with my box of historical design and décor books. There was no time to waste if I was going to impress Prince Reynard.

Chapter 6

Calder

Well, I'd made a jerk of myself last night.

I pushed the two-by-four through the compound miter saw and made the sawdust fly. It smelled good. Lots better than a high school classroom, no matter how many windows I kept open.

But I had a good reason for being a jerk. Mallory's ten-fast-facts responses had been far too suspicious for me to not react badly—considering every single one of them hit on exactly the same themes as Alanis's lies.

I love small towns.

I am fascinated by history and architecture and combined them into a career.

My dream is to go to Greece and Rome to see the ancient ruins.

I love reading long history books.

Alanis's very answers! Alanis, my so-called perfect match.

Those lies had fooled me completely. I'd been dragged along in a haze of love-blindness until I'd bought a ring, planned my proposal speech, talked to her father to ask his permission.

Bile crept up my throat.

Fortunately, her façade had crumbled on that fated Christmas morning three years ago. If not, my life would look horrifically different right now: divorced, my parents' company decimated, a laughingstock for being duped by a gorgeous female con artist and her scheming family.

Alanis. Liar to her core. Plus, she hadn't even been a brunette! The silken dark hair had been nothing but an expensive wig over her dirty-blonde mop. Worse, she wasn't even Irish! Alanis O'Houlihan was her *stage name.*

The woman had planted C4 in my heart and detonated it into smithereens.

Forever.

Small towns are the best.

History and architecture are my passion. I'm combining them into a career.

I'd love to visit Greece and Rome, with all the ancient ruins.

I love stopping at historical markers on long drives.

My reaction was justifiable, right? Mallory Jameson's uncannily identical responses had to have been planned. Cold climbed my spine just reviewing them.

Alanis's lies had been confirmed by her father when she took me to the Irish wake for her grandmother to meet her family.

They hadn't even been her family! Instead, they'd all been hired actors, buddies of her dad's—all in on the deception.

There hadn't even been a death. It was a fake-wake for my benefit. Er, detriment.

I'd soaked it all in. A sponge of total naïveté.

Never again.

Except, Mallory Jameson was a hundred times better at acting than Alanis had been. In fact, she'd seemed completely sincere. In fact, half of me believed her, even in the light of day.

With Alanis there'd always been a hint of flippancy, a note of arch superiority when we were together—which I'd found attractive, even irresistible, at the time.

More's the pity.

"There." I took the board, now transformed into a length of baseboard. "How's that?" I leaned it up against the wall, just as Mallory walked in.

"It's really great, but ..."

"But?"

"But it's not mahogany."

"We'll stain it."

"And it's not Georgian in style."

"Yes, it is."

"No, it's not." She patted a textbook under her arm. "I could show you, if you like."

I didn't need to be schooled by this imposter. "I think I've done enough remodels in my time to know what homeowners like." And they liked my handiwork. Every time. Sure, I may have pretended not to like being involved in Mom and Dad's side business of restorations, but I took pride in my craftsmanship. "My baseboards are impeccable."

"If you're doing Arts and Crafts style of the nineteen twenties, yes." She waved off my excellent board like it was nothing. "But we need to rewind to about a century earlier, pal."

"Pal?" Of all the nicknames.

"My boss insists that we become pals." She gave a little shrug and a toss of that gorgeous dark chestnut hair. It gleamed even without the aid of candlelight or moonlight. "So, I'm calling you pal."

"No, you're not."

"Fine." She flipped open her book. "See? Georgian."

Oh. Definitely much more ornate than what I'd created. Not discounting my creation at all, of course. "That is not going to fit the design of this house."

"Ya think?" She sighed and put the book back under her arm. "Of all the mismatched designs in this house, Georgian is the only style he shouldn't have chosen."

I lowered my voice. "Do you think he even knows what Georgian means?"

"Don't doubt the prince, pal." She pushed her lips out at me like a cartoon duck. "Quack."

"Quack, quack," I said back.

The mood lightened.

"Fine." She heaved a sigh. "What are we going to do? To make this place Georgian, which requires symmetry and mirrored architecture, we are going to need more than woodwork."

No kidding. This place needed a gutting anyway, but I didn't have time for that. "What do you say we go look at the local homes, any that are open for tours? We can check out what they're like, take some snaps, and then come back and show the prince our ideas."

"Our ideas? I'm supposed to be the legislative branch and you're the executive branch. You execute and implement my ideas. Which are law."

"You do realize that the head of the executive branch is the president. The Founders planned it that way."

"Founders." She pushed my shoulder a little. "Fine. You can make some suggestions."

She'd touched me. It took me a second to recover.

"Suggestions it is. I'll drive." We went out to my truck. "This had better not take us too long. Every day burns through a box on the calendar. I don't have time to waste."

"When does school start?"

"How did—?" I let my foot off the gas for a second.

"Rochelle told me."

"My mom doesn't like that I teach." I resumed my speed.

"Your mom? Rochelle is your mom?"

Oh, geez. What had I done? If on the off-chance Mallory hadn't pre-researched my identity as the heir of Royal Construction, I'd blown it. I had exactly one cat in the bag—a ravenous tiger—and I'd just let it out with the most casual drop of a word.

Unless she didn't know that my parents owned Royal Construction.

She had to know. Everyone knew.

"Yeah, I'm their son." My mind scampered for some log to float me before I drowned. "They rope me into these remodeling projects every holiday."

I kept my eyes on the road, but my peripheral vision took in her every reaction. What Mallory said next would tell me everything about what she'd known and what her gold-digging intentions were.

"Oh, how sad. You probably never find time to read as much as you'd like to."

The steering wheel jerked to the right for a second. I righted it. "Sorry." The sympathy on exactly the core topic of my heart had taken me aback. "Yeah, reading. Life is way too short for my TBR pile."

"What are you reading now?"

I told her about Alexander the Great. "What about you?" This would tell me a lot.

"I just got the new Jake Travers release on the Battle of the Bulge, but I haven't had time to dig into it yet. That's another place I'd like to see—the Ardennes forest in Belgium. My great-grandfather fought there."

"He was at the deciding battle of World War II?"

"Yeah. He made it home, but he never talked about it, my dad said. It's always held a morbid fascination for me, and I can't seem to get my hands on enough material about it." She tossed a few facts at me about German tanks, hills, battle strategy, and pure divine intervention at that battle.

"You really do know a lot about it." I'd taught it in World War II courses, but never with that level of detail.

She glanced down at her phone and then up at the road. "Here's Evergreen Point. Take a right at this turnoff. It's a home open for tours starting at nine o'clock. We'll be first in line."

I wheeled my truck onto the evergreen-tree-lined asphalt. At its

34

end was a Gilded Age mansion worthy of being down the coast. "Good thing these people built far enough away from Newport to not be in competition with The Breakers or The Elms." The titans of industry's summer "cottages" were legendary.

"This is quite the mansion. Should be called Evergreen *Palace*, not Evergreen Point. And check it out. It's designed in Federal style, which is close to Georgian." Mallory alighted from the truck, and we crossed the pea-gravel parking lot toward a manicured lawn area, ringed with firs and spruces. "I bet it costs a fortune to heat and cool."

Out came a docent. "Yes, darlings. It's more than a fortune. Luckily, Mr. Delacourt has the family chocolate fortune to keep the temperature inside comfortable year-round. Let me take your coats."

"Oh, that's where I've heard the name Delacourt," Mallory whispered when the woman took our jackets to a cloakroom. "Those chocolates were amazing. I used to love them. They seemed a little different-tasting these days. Not quite as good as when I was a kid."

The hostess returned and bowed to us. "Now, then. I'm Dulcie Delacourt-Tremaine, cousin to Mr. Delacourt, who is tending to business in the city. My husband and I are in residence while Mr. Delacourt is away, and I'll be happy to take you on a guided tour of our family home and grounds."

I dug a few dollars out of my pocket for our admission fee, but she refused it. "We do this as a service to the community, but only when Mr. Delacourt is not here." Dulcie gave me a regal nod, and we walked inside to where a reception desk stood. "Please, take as many pictures as you like for your personal use, but don't put them on any kind of internet site. There's a waiver for you to sign about that." She pushed a paper at us, and we signed it, but then we brought our phones' cameras to the ready.

Mallory reached over and squeezed my hand. In my ear, she whispered, "I can't believe we're seeing this house in real life. I hadn't realized it's in Seacliff. I thought it sat farther up the coast. It's much less commercialized than so many of the other houses from the era."

She whispered a half dozen facts about the fine example of Federal architecture—fluted Corinthian columns, Palladian windows, all inspired by ancient Greece and Rome.

Even though in this moment, it seemed I'd misjudged her, I'd wait and see. Fool me once, shame on you. Fool me twice ...

We trailed along behind the guide.

"As you can see, the fireplace is symmetrical with delicate details at the mantel ..." Dulcie Delacourt-Tremaine went on about details of the house, and I dutifully snapped a few pictures of the much-touted mantel and the chair rail, but Mallory Jameson had my full attention.

Was she for real?

You don't know anything about me.

Well, I intended to.

Chapter 7

Mallory

"You didn't seem all that interested in the Delacourt place, not even in the sixteen species of evergreen trees surrounding the park." I climbed into the truck. For whatever reason, Calder had gotten the door for me. Maybe because now I knew who his mom was—and he worried I'd rat him out if he didn't act like a gentleman. "Why don't you choose our next stop?"

"I liked it okay." He closed me inside and came around to drive. "What about Flame Cottage?" he asked absently. He was focused on something else. I glanced over as he started the truck.

His eyes were on me.

He righted them and looked at the road.

"I know Flame Cottage. Is it nearby?" It had been in all of my design books. From what I'd heard, it contained several examples of Duncan Phyfe furniture—the highest quality of its time, along with Chippendale.

"I saw on the map that it isn't too far up the coastline. We'll pass a few lighthouses."

"Do you like lighthouses?" I hated them. "Don't you think there's something ominous and creepy about them. A harbinger of doom?"

"What are you talking about?" Calder steered us back onto the main road. "Everyone loves lighthouses. They keep sailors safe."

"They make a creepy clicking sound, and you know they wouldn't have put one there if a lot of boats hadn't crashed and people drowned. They're *ghost lights*." Why was I telling Calder Kimball about my deep-seated fear of lighthouses? "Never mind. I'm probably the only one."

On the steering wheel, Calder's knuckles flexed. "No, I like that you're not trying to be a generic people-pleaser. Go ahead and tell me all your unpopular opinions."

"Seriously? And let you in on what a freak I am for disliking modern art and wishing everything ever painted by flicks of paint instead of actual effort could be taken to the bottom of the sea by a millstone? No, thanks."

"What you're saying, so delicately, is you hate modern art."

I made a gagging sound.

"I get that," he said matter-of-factly. "It's valid."

"Really? You hate it, too?" The word finally registered in my mind. "But, isn't it *avant garde* to love modern art and all things from the nineteen fifties these days?"

"The only thing I actually like from that era, including the music, is the Kit-Cat clock."

I clasped my shirt's hem, gripping it hard. "The black and white clock with the cat eyes that look back and forth every second that ticks by?" I loved those!

"With the tail as pendulum." He shrugged. "Invented by Earl Arnault in the nineteen thirties. Early examples have a metal body." He looked as if he could wax on but stopped himself. "Yeah. Those have a kitschy appeal for me I can't account for."

"I agree. Almost everything else from that decade on is … lacking."

"What about George Nakashima? The furniture designer?" he asked, apparently a fan. Luckily, I was, too.

"No, he's different. I consider him a throwback to a time of greater insight. He fits more in the Frank Lloyd Wright pattern of ingenuity for me."

For the rest of the drive up the coast, we went on about different furniture designers, from the Stickley brothers of the turn of the 20th century to Louis Comfort Tiffany—who Calder knew had also designed furniture and not just jewelry. Or lamps.

The time flew by. And I didn't even get creeped out by the lighthouse when we passed it. Calder kept my mind off it.

In fact, talking to him wasn't nearly as bad as I'd expected after the catastrophe of our seaside walk. He really did stink at small talk. Talking about work was much better—and gave me a lot more insight into who he really was than if he'd rattled off a list of facts.

We pulled up at Flame Cottage.

"Whoa." My breath whooshed out of me. "This place is enormous. The photos don't do it justice."

"Photos? Do you already know about this place?"

"It's one of the examples from a bunch I chose for my master's thesis." I gawped at it as we crossed yet another pea-gravel parking lot, lined with animal-shaped topiaries.

"Then you know the owners imported entire ceilings from European castles to place inside."

"Just like William Randolph Hearst did out on the California coast." I suspected Hearst had gotten the idea from the owners of Flame Cottage. "Wasn't there a fire, though?"

"Burned thirty percent of the interior, but the exterior remained intact." He held the front door open for me. "I think they should've named it something else."

"Right? They thought they jinxed themselves."

"Maybe they should've rechristened it when they rebuilt." I climbed the porch steps in some kind of floating daze, like I was entering an oft-recurring dream. "Whoa. It's beautiful."

Calder held the door for me again, and we went into the soaring foyer, filled with European and African art, an eclectic mix. It smelled like ginger and eastern spices. The floor's tiles shone reflectively. It was even better than my books had promised.

"Do we just walk through?" Calder picked up a pamphlet and a pair of headsets for us. The tour was self-guided but with an audio recording that told us both things we already knew. After a bit, we simply stopped listening to the voice with the clipped Continental accent. So Eurotrash-esque.

We passed through bedroom after bedroom with curtained canopy beds, wall tapestries, and libraries with more art than books.

"I feel like I'm back in the Pitti Palace in Florence." Calder let me pass through the doorway first.

"You've been to Florence?" I sighed and stepped into yet another soaring room—this time with a tray ceiling. "You're so lucky."

His brows pushed together. "Yeah, I guess I am."

"I'd love to see the Ufizzi Galleries. Oh, and the David statue!"

Calder snorted. "Every woman wants to see the David statue."

"Not in that way. Geez." I still wanted to see it in real life. I'd heard it was much more impressive in person. "Just because you've been there, you can't belittle my wish to see history on display, too."

His chin wrinkled. "I didn't mean it that way. I agree—everyone should see Florence. The outer walls, the gates, the Duomo, the Piazza de Santo Spirito. It's history. You should see it."

"Sounds like you know all the right places to see."

Whatever openness had been in Calder's countenance up to that point closed off, *whammo!* As in, *shields up, Captain!*

"I'm not taking you to Italy." His eyes were steel.

Oh, brother. My eyes rolled so hard I think they scratched my cerebral cortex. "The last person I want to tour Italy with is you." I'd be going with a prince when I went. Someone for whom a simple tour through the various provinces would never make the slightest dent in

40

his bank account. We could stay on the shores of Lake Como in his summer palace eating gelato and gnocchi, and …

"What is that weird, dreamy look you just got?"

My stomach growled. "Italian food. The thought makes me dreamy." Maybe Prince Reynard and I could ride a scooter together with my arms around his waist.

"I'll tell you one thing—Italian pizza isn't all it's cracked up to be. Anchovies pollute way too much of it."

"I like anchovies."

"Maybe so, but Americans took the pizza idea and perfected it."

Pizza-banter calmed him down. I'd have to remember that. "You're just being contrary." But I did need lunch. "Let's go back and eat. I think we have a few ideas and photos we can draw on for design inspiration for Prince Reynard."

Prince Reynard. The only guy on this job I should be sharing travel banter and pizza banter with—whether Calder Kimball was a school teacher or construction worker like Dylan.

I'd better keep that in mind.

Chapter 8

Calder

Every hour I spent with Mallory Jameson felt like a seesaw. One second I was flying high, the next I was clunking back to the ground, bruising my tailbone.

Was she doing it on purpose? One second she acted like she wanted me to lavish her with vacations and European tours, and then the next second she told me—*point blank*—that I was the last man on earth she'd want to go to Europe with.

She gave me a headache. And mysteriously, my tailbone hurt, too. Existential psychosomatic problems.

I blamed Mallory.

"Oh, Prince Reynard." Mallory spied him as we pulled into the circular drive of Buckworth Castle. "I'm going to go catch him and see what he thinks of these ideas we collected." She jumped out before I even had the truck out of gear.

"Wait—we haven't synthesized ..." Synthesized? What, I was an '80s musical instrument now? "No, never mind."

"Come on, Calder. You snapped some of the better example photos."

I slammed my door and trounced after her. "Excuse me, Prince

Reynard. She's enthusiastic."

"I love her enthusiasm." That weird gleam came into his eye again, the same one as when he'd been watching her eat. "It's infectious. Contagious? Which do you say more correctly in English, I wonder?"

The term I would have used was irrational. Irrational enthusiasm.

Prince Reynard didn't hang on my reply. Nor did Mallory. In fact, it would appear she was hanging on the prince's words instead.

A weird sludge rolled over me, though it shouldn't! I shouldn't be reacting. Who cared whether Mallory Jameson flirted with that greasy dude from across the sea? Not me.

Nuh-uh. He could have her. I was done with women. Especially women at the holidays.

The sludge was only because I wasn't used to playing second fiddle to guys worse-looking than me, not jealousy. Just ... me being a fish out of water, to use the phrase Chaucer coined.

"Do you like this one, Prince?" Mallory swiped through photos on her phone, sharing the view of her screen with him, standing with her shoulder touching his. "Or do you think this one is nicer?"

The slide show went on, and then Mallory borrowed my phone and scrolled the pictures from our mansion visits. I stood there wishing I had some gum to chew or a book to read, while Reynard grunted his approval at literally every single photograph.

"I like this. All of it."

All of it? The ceilings at the second place had been gaudy, though.

Mallory batted her eyes at him. "We could make it look like all of this, except better."

"Better?" His head snapped upward, and he bored a hole through her with his stare. "That's exactly what I want. Better than all those."

Ah, competitive, was he? I could work with that—in fact, it was our ticket out of the Big Top world. I stepped forward.

"Sure, we can," I said confidently. With "better" as our guiding star, we could knock out this job in six weeks. Tick-tock, tick-tock. Like the pendulum tail of the Kit-Cat clock measured, time was wasting.

"You can do this, yes?" He ignored me and looked at Mallory.

She nodded, her doe-eyes wide, liquid, almost adoring.

A frisson vibrated across my skin.

"However," I said, gathering myself, "we'll have to make some major decisions." Like whether to gut the place down to its terrible studs and start fresh.

"No, no. I don't want decisions." He waved me back. "I want exactly what she's saying: *better*. Better than Evergreen Point or Flame Cottage."

Bingo! She'd done it!

"You got it, Prince Reynard." Mallory held up a hand for him to high-five.

The prince high-fived her. It looked weird. Her eyes were bright. Mine narrowed.

"Do you have a budget in mind?" Why were my teeth clenched?

Prince Reynard kept his eyes trained on Mallory. "Carte blanche. Spend anything you need." He reached into his jacket's inner pocket and handed Mallory something from inside.

Well, well. Now I couldn't care less that he'd ignored me entirely. He'd just passed Mallory a black American Express Card. We were in business! And with carte blanche—or was that *carte noir*?—we could do anything we wanted at any rate we wanted.

"Would you like to accompany me out to my car, Miss Jameson?" the prince asked, offering her his arm. However, before she could accept and sashay away with him, he received a phone call. The doofus held up a finger and then left her standing there in the room.

I wouldn't say she looked disappointed, exactly. Devastated, smashed on the rocks of a shore without a lighthouse was more like it.

"Good job," I said.

"Yeah. Thanks." Her voice was flat. "I guess we need to draw up some plans. I'll work on some, you work on some, and we'll meet up after supper?" She didn't wait for me to respond, just headed out the

44

back door of Buckworth Castle toward where the cottages lay.

For a second, I considered following her to offer to collaborate, but she obviously didn't want company. Instead, I ended up heading out the front door, where Prince Reynard was yelling loudly.

"I said I'll get you the money, which means I'll get you the money. Aish! What is this, some kind of mafia shakedown?" He wasn't trying to conceal his voice at all, but I tried not to listen. "I'm not a criminal. I'm good for the debts."

This wasn't my business. At least not beyond the question of whether or not Mom and Dad's company would be paid in a timely manner for their work.

As long as the AmEx Card doesn't get slapped with a limit, it's not my problem.

I turned around to walk away. Fast.

Before I could get out of earshot, however, he yelled more. "Casinos like yours should be burned to the ground. No, that's not a threat of arson. Who do you think I am, some thug like you? I'm a prince. We do not commit arson to get out of gambling debts. We are gentlemen. We pay them when our fathers agree to fork over the money. And I'm working on him. Trust me. Yes, thank you for being so much calmer now. You have my personal guarantee. Yes, sir, it *is* worth something." He stomped toward his luxury sedan in the drive. The car kicked up gravel as he tore away.

A roiling sickness gurgled upward through my digestive system.

However, this time I knew why.

I can't let Mallory be involved with that man.

Chapter 9

Mallory

We sat on a bench overlooking the ocean from atop the cliff at the edge of Buckworth's property. Waves crested white and broke in early-winter anger, as if reflecting Calder's glowering mood.

"I don't know why you're being so reluctant to make decisions this morning." I wanted to push Calder off the edge of that cliffside walk again, he was being so stubborn, and he'd ditched me last night at dinner. "Aren't we facing a ticking clock? You're the one with school starting again."

"Oh. Right." Calder aimed his eyes back down at my drawings. "The prince will like these, and then we can finish transforming Buckworth and get back to our lives." He sent a pointed look at me. "*Our* lives."

Huh. The guy was being super weird. He paced the ground in front of my viewing bench.

He'd been so excited when Prince Reynard first handed me the credit card and offered to let us buy everything we needed for the project. What had happened to him while I was making plans for the Gilded Age remodel? Even at dinnertime Calder had been moody and monosyllabic. There'd even been an upset grunt.

"What are you keeping from me?" I might as well ask, since we were stuck doing this, and we couldn't go forward if he was in this mood. "Spill it, pal."

"Pal? Again?" He looked up. In this light, Calder looked ruggedly handsome, like when I'd first mistaken him for a prince. "It's nothing. I mean—it's something, but I don't really want to talk about it right now."

"Did your girlfriend call and give you bad news of some kind?"

Ugh. Where had the girlfriend reference come from? This was not an oblique way of pumping him for private relationship information. I did not care whether he had a girlfriend.

I'm so lame.

His head popped up. "I don't have a girlfriend!" It came out sharp, lethal.

Of course, if he happened to tell me anyway, I'd take it. But I'd rather it came in nicer packaging. Sheesh. "Fine. Sorry." Touchy! The breakup must still be fresh on his soul, apparently. "I didn't mean … never mind. Can we just focus on this and get started? We have a lot of work to do. Basically, we need to redesign every inch of the nine thousand square feet in that monstrosity. Three floors, plus the stairwell to the cupola. Not to mention a reworking of the exterior, so that it doesn't look like it was designed by a committee who never agreed or made concessions. I'm a historical preservation expert, not a designer, too. It's a challenge. I can copy, but I'm not sure I create from scratch, so I'd love it if you'd focus."

Normally, I didn't want a *team* giving me input, but in this case, I was at sea. I needed someone like Calder who cared about historical accuracy plus the incentive of his parents' reputation being on the line.

"Look, if you're worried, we could just bring in Mom and Dad's professional design team, and you could direct. They're on retainer. They do this stuff all the time."

"Unfortunately, no. I tried floating that plan to Prince Reynard already, and he was pretty insistent on my ideas driving the design." One thing about Reynard, he was easy to read, his every emotion showing on his face.

Calder's mouth crumpled and a deep line formed between his brows. "The prince," he practically spat.

Hey. Don't bite the hand that feeds you, underpaid school teacher. "What do you have against Prince Reynard? He's our paycheck right now, and he's been pretty gracious about acquiescing to our suggestions about the design. At least we're not stuck trying to fix what was there. We should be grateful we're not dealing with someone impossible. Trust me, I've dealt with impossible clients in the past. The prince is not one of them."

In fact, he was kind of charming. And his smile was really growing on me. When he looked at me, it was like he was fascinated by a rare tropical fish. We'd had one true conversation now—the first of many, I hoped. If I played things right, I could probably wrangle a dinner meeting out of him.

Was I attractive enough to catch his eye? I didn't have much else to offer besides my charm or my gratitude for his notice of me. He might be the type to fall for a woman who lavished him with praise and attention. Someone who worshiped him.

I could be that woman.

Or, if he preferred a woman who challenged him, I could try to become that match for him. Or whatever he needed.

What I needed was a prince. Correction, what I'd wished for was a prince, back during that first snowfall with my friends. What I *needed* was food security.

"It's not that, Mallory." Calder paced the turf. "There's something off about him is all."

No, there wasn't. Everything was a jolly holiday with Prince Reynard. It was Calder who had mood whiplash.

"Let's just get to work." I aimed my drawings at him again. This time he focused his attention. "So, I came up with a few ideas for a cohesive time-period design set squarely in the Edwardian era. Check these out and tell me if they're possible to implement in the time and space we have." Having zero budget constraints was the best. "No matter what we choose, we do have one constraint: make it better than Evergreen Point or Flame Cottage."

Calder flopped down next to me. Wow, he smelled good when he was fresh from a morning shower, a mixture of sawdust and Irish Spring. I exhaled hard to get the scent out of my senses so I could focus—on the plans and on my potential prince.

If we wowed Prince Reynard, he'd trust me more, maybe even look my way.

Just like I'm looking Calder's way right now.

Gah! I refocused on my designs.

"Oh, hey. I found something last night." Calder pulled out his phone. "Check it out."

But he hadn't evaluated my designs yet! I looked anyway, and— gulp! "Is that"—I swallowed my gum—"Buckworth Castle?" I took the phone and looked closer at the screen shots. The exterior was the same overall square shape, but the cupola I couldn't deny as being identical.

"While you and Prince Reginald were dreaming up plans—"

"You mean *Reynard.* Not Reginald."

"While you were dreaming—I did a little fact-finding mission to the local historical society. They were open until nine. This was the original footprint of the mansion, and this is how the interior and exterior looked."

"These aren't from the seventies." I swiped through the pictures on his screen. "No avocado or Harvest Gold appliances here. These pictures have got to be over a hundred years old." They looked to be circa 1890. "Where did you get this again? Are you sure it's Buckworth Castle?"

But it obviously was. The views were identical. Some of the landscaping—albeit overgrown now—was still the same, and the cliff was undeniably the cliff overlooking the sea from this spot. And, there was the cupola.

"It's different, right?"

None of the fake turrets, widow's walk, bay windows. None of the Victorian gingerbread, no ghastly additions in helter-skelter styles. In fact … "It was really quite charming. Is that stucco beneath the siding and the rock façade?" I'd seen the pink stucco peeking through on my first day here. These were black and white snaps, but … "It *could be* the same place."

"Yep. Now, check out the pictures of the interior."

They were even better. The place oozed with charm—rather than oozing with ooze.

"This is amazing!" It was exactly our answer! "You did it! You saved this project!" Caught up in the moment, I threw my arms around Calder's neck. Even faster, I sprang back. "Sorry. I didn't mean to …"

He had a weird look on his face, kind of like the one Mowgli wore when he first saw the girl going to fetch the water. But it quickly disappeared, and he straightened up.

"Well." Calder cleared his throat. "You're not the only one who can do historical research for this project."

I cringed. He'd done what I should have done in the first place and dug around locally, rather than making assumptions or leaps and guesses. Calder had me discombobulated. I mean, the prince did.

"Let's get cracking." I jumped up. "I can tell at a glance that we'll need to order a lot of materials, but we also need to get going on demolition."

"My parents' crew can start that, if we give them a detailed design plan for returning to the original layout—plus plumbing and electrical, of course. Oh, and first things first—the inland-facing façade must go."

"First thing." I couldn't agree more. "Hey, how deeply did you look into the original design?"

"Medium. They closed before I could really dive in."

"Sometimes historical societies will archive actual blueprints of important buildings." Energy surged in me. "I wonder …"

"Should we go check?"

We? He wanted to come along for the research? "What time do they open?"

***

An hour later, we were up to our necks in historically accurate details about Buckworth Castle's original state. Every inch of it had begun as a lovely, delightful home overlooking the Atlantic coast.

"In its infancy, it was practically a chateau." Swoon! Two stories, symmetrical, overlooking the sea. It had four windows on each wing of the house, with a central section that bumped out like a bay window, but which looked cogent to the original design. It was gorgeous! These photos were also black and white, but even so, I could swear the original coloring was a blushy pink.

"That was its original name, you know. The Seacliff Chateau. The first owners used it as a summer home to escape the heat of New York City."

Seacliff Chateau. That was perfect. So much more fitting than Buckworth Castle. "Can I be candid? I love it. This version of that home calls to my heart. I can't wait to give it back its dignity and beauty. Calder, we have to. The original deserves that respect."

Calder's gaze met my eyes. He searched them. "I ... I feel the same way." Passion laced his voice. Passion for the project, I mean. Of course. He wasn't looking at *me* with those passionate gazes. They were for the building.

Energy surged between us. "We're doing this, then?" My breath caught.

"Together." Calder ran a sensual finger down the photograph, and my skin shivered. "Because—look. I love my parents, but they want to make every single thing modern. It's been their whole business focus until this project. There's a reason they hired you as their historical consultant, Mallory—and part of it was to keep them from making huge mistakes and getting lawsuits slapped on them by a local historical society busybody."

"That actually happened? Really?" Rochelle and Darren hadn't mentioned it. "How awful."

"Just once, but they were able to amend the situation until the angry person was appeased." He rubbed his thumb against his fingertips indicating it had cost them a pretty penny. "Which means, you're their insurance."

"Your parents are so nice. I'll do everything I can to keep them from going through that again."

But how?

I put my brain on it.

For one, I could start by cozying up to the local historical society. I'd put that on my to-do list for another day. Today we had final photos to examine and consider. I picked up a new stash.

Oh, my goodness! "Look at this stack of Christmas pictures!" Every inch of the castle was decked out in holiday splendor. I pushed them toward Calder so he could check them out, but he shook his head.

"What's wrong?"

"Nothing." He had averted his eyes. The ceiling was now the most important thing in the room. Followed by the floor. And a framed certificate on the wall.

"Liar." I waited. He clammed up. I waited some more.

Calder cracked first. "I just don't think the Christmastime photos are going to help us restore the house is all. There's too much clutter."

"Uh, in case you haven't noticed, at the very soul of Christmas lives *clutter*." I made sparkle-fingers. "At least in all the Christmases you see on TV. Every inch of a true Christmas home is jam-packed with boughs and baubles." It hadn't been that way in my house growing up. We were lucky to get one gift, and we never had a tree or a roast anything. "Come on. Up until a second ago you were gung-ho. One Christmas photo and you get cold feet?"

Calder set down the file and looked me in the eye. "What if I told you I don't really like Christmas?"

Chapter 10

Calder

The look of horror would dawn on Mallory's face any second now, after my Terrible Confession.

A Christmas-hater, an inch from her arm, breathing her same air. Her lip would curl and her nose would turn up.

"Why?" No disgust marred her tone. "It's Christmas."

I wasn't telling her why. That was my cross to bear. Alone.

"Let's go walk around outside." Mallory grabbed my elbow and took me out the door and down the steps of the old Victorian house that served as the local historical repository. "You need some air."

I did. But how could Mallory tell? Was I pale or something?

Still, she was right about my need for crisp air. Every time I thought about Christmas anymore, my lungs got stuffy.

We strolled down the sidewalk, passed a few houses and businesses, and headed toward a bakery. Its smells were tendrils of deliciousness tugging me inside.

Mallory must have been drawn to the baking scents, too, because she paused at the door. "Hungry?"

"Not until I smelled the yeast and flour."

"Same." She went in. I must have followed her. At the counter, she ordered two hot cocoas and a pair of cranberry scones. My head stopped swimming, and I didn't need to hold onto the countertop by the time the baker brought out our order.

Then, the cringe-inducing sight whacked me: the shop was bedecked with holiday decorations—something I'd avoided seeing for the past couple of years, since St. Dominic's never bothered with decking the halls with students and faculty gone over the long break, and Mom and Dad could hardly adorn their holiday remodels with seasonal trappings.

If I'd been immature, I would have shielded my eyes from the red and green plaid bunting draped everywhere.

"I asked for a shot of mint in my cocoa. Do you want to try it?" Mallory offered me her cup as we headed toward a table near the window. "I got raspberry for yours. I hope that's okay. What's wrong? Are you hiding from someone? Why do you have your hands over the sides of your eyes like a horse with blinders?"

So I was immature.

We sat. I took my hands down and lifted the cocoa to sip. "Mmm. I love raspberry." And this raspberry was better than any other I'd tasted in a while. "It goes well with hot cocoa." The hot drink trailed down my throat, settling the shiver in my belly. "Thanks."

"Do you want to talk about it?"

No. Yes. No. "Haven't you read about Mars and Venus, how—unlike women—men don't like to talk about their issues?"

"Of course I have. But I'm guessing you've been in your cave for awhile. If you're ready, feel free to come on out. No pressure, though."

Instead of a high-pressure stare-down, like I would've expected, Mallory simply looked out at the foot traffic passing on the sidewalk. She didn't even make small talk.

She was a unique woman.

I gulped the too-hot cocoa. Ouch! It burned all the way down. Lesson learned, I dipped the edge of the scone in it, soaking it before taking a bite. "Good scone."

"Mmm. Delicious. Mmm. It's a good thing I don't live in Seacliff. I'd get as big as the cliff itself." She took another bite, following my scone-dipping lead. "Good life-hack. Thanks." She ate another bite, this time with relish. "This is amazing." She let out a long, satisfied sigh.

"Why do you eat so enthusiastically?" I mean, the scones were good, but not noise-making-level good.

With a casual shrug, she set her food down. "I guess when you grow up not knowing when your next meal will be—or even if this one will be taken away mid-bite—you get into bad habits."

"As in …?"

"As in shoveling down spoonfuls and over-stating how delicious it is in hopes that whoever provided it will give you more. Just in case there's extra in the kitchen. Maybe some to take with you to hedge against the gnawing stomach of the following day or days."

All of this she delivered with complete nonchalance. Could she really mean it? "Did you actually go hungry as a child?"

She patted her hips. "I'll never be like other women who complain that they're fat. These curves are hard-won. They're protection against famine."

Famine. Who even thought about famine these days, at least around here? "Mallory, that's really tough."

"It was. But once I was old enough, I worked a couple or three jobs—always one in a restaurant that offered at least one meal per shift. Then I got a meal a day, guaranteed."

I probably looked like the Blinking Guy meme. "You're serious."

"It's not exactly comedy routine material, hunger." She took another bite of her scone. "But if it makes you uncomfortable, I'll try to pace myself and keep my food-appreciation-sounds to a minimum. No guarantee that the behavior won't crop up again. But I promise to try, okay?"

"No, no." I pushed my scone toward her, as if it could fly in a time machine to her younger self. "Do you want mine?"

"I mean, yes, but you go ahead." She grinned at me. "Although, if you get partway through and can't finish it, don't throw it away."

I might never leave an uneaten grain of rice on a plate again as long as I lived. "Mallory, I had no idea."

"Why would you?" Again with the little nonchalant shrug. "We all have things about our pasts that we don't wear on our sleeves. Things that make us act in ways that would seem weird to other people."

My voice lowered a notch. "Like disliking Christmas, you mean?"

"That wasn't what I was getting at, but sure." She poked at my cup. "That's a pretty timely example."

There was my cue. Could I tell her? I weighed it. I took another sip. I looked at Mallory, who wasn't staring me down but had turned her attention to the sidewalk shoppers again, as if to give me space to consider.

Or, was it for some other reason?

She's not into me. She's a coworker. All that stuff that sounded just like Alanis wasn't made up. She actually does like history. And she might be into the prince—unfortunately. If I don't give her my trust, I can't gain hers. And then, she won't trust me if I tell her what the prince is up to.

"Three years ago"—I cleared my throat. I cleared it again. A whole army of frogs had moved in. It took me another couple of tries before finally I could speak—"three years ago, I was engaged at Christmas."

"Oh." Mallory set down her cup. "It didn't work out."

"Not at all." Should I tell her more? "My fiancée wasn't the person I had been led to believe she was." Did that begin to convey the depth of Alanis's deception? No, but it covered the basics.

I watched for Mallory's response. Would she be like Mom and Dad and tell me I was wrong to let that liar go?

"That must have been really hard." Mallory took her last bite, clearly thinking as she chewed. She swallowed and then spoke. "Being misled is tough to get over. It taints everything, makes you assume everyone is secretly tricking you."

My eyes widened. "Right?" I tried to sound nonchalant to match her tone, but astonishment intensified my response. This woman had encapsulated my feelings perfectly. It took me a second to breathe right, and then I said, "After it happened, for a year, I kept looking over my shoulder, expecting to see some kind of *Truman Show* camera, filming my life. I had this sneaking feeling everything in my world was just a movie set, and I was just the center of a great hoax."

Mallory pushed her plate aside, rested her elbows on the table, and placed her chin on her hands. "I totally know that feeling." Her eyes were deep, like pools of truth. "In fact, I suspect we're all secretly afraid we're on the *Truman Show*. Except, for me, it's the *Mallory Show*." She took a slow sip of her cocoa, gazing at me over the rim of her mug. "How are you now? Getting better?"

No. I mean—well, I hadn't been. Alanis's face flashed up in my memory. She wore her usual taunting grin and her dirty blonde hair was askew, like she'd looked when I accused her of fraud and she'd ripped off her brunette wig to mock me.

Yet, for whatever reason, the sting was duller in this moment. It hadn't gone away entirely, but the blade's tip wasn't as sharp.

I blinked to clear the image, and the face of Mallory Jameson was sitting before me—with her authentically kind eyes, her naturally chestnut brown hair, and her sincere caring.

"A little better, I think." With hope for more improvement to come.

Chapter 11

Mallory

A full week of demolition commenced. Walls that didn't need to be there tumbled into dusty heaps. Stones to make the place look medieval were hauled away in big metal roll-off containers. Enough landscaping was cleared to use the lumber to build a whole housing development.

A broad view of the ocean opened up, and an ellipse was prepared for sod to be laid next spring. The place would be gorgeous—and look just like the pictures of its original glory, right down to the pink stucco that appeared on the seaside face of the building once the trees were removed.

Prince Reynard had made himself scarce since our one big conversation—the one I'd hoped would lead to many more. Nope. We had not become the Texting BFFs I'd fantasized about. He'd turned the project over to me with no micromanagement from his side, or even input.

For all I knew, had gone back to Europe.

What did he do in Europe with all his free time? Probably visited the poor and widowed and orphaned. Frequented convalescent hospitals. Attended charity functions to save the rainforests or something equally noble.

I mean, no. That was more wishful thinking. Reynard didn't have much of an aura of being noble, but he was a prince, so that counted as nobility, right?

One afternoon, I returned to my bungalow to grab a sweatshirt. The weather was getting colder. I pushed open the door.

"Oh, my lands!" I fell against the doorframe. *One, two, three ... nine, ten ... fifteen, sixteen.* Twenty or more flower vases sat on every flat surface, and each was filled with dozens of red roses. "Where did all these come from?" I asked it aloud, even though no one else was around to answer.

Was I imagining it? No. I pinched myself hard. I was awake. Finally, I set foot in the bungalow—and went from bouquet to bouquet, inhaling the rose scent. Roses! In all colors! I loved roses. Who didn't?

"What's the holdup?" Calder poked his head into the bungalow. "You were coming right back, and—" He looked around. "Are those real? You might have a flower hoarding problem."

"Can you come in and shut the door?" The cold might spoil the flowers. Or could it? I didn't know. And—who'd sent these?

Except, I knew. Finally, a small card appeared. *For Mallory. –R*

Reynard! Clavicle-clasp! I hugged the card to my heart. I needed to thank him. If only I had his number.

Calder, watching, must have read the whole situation. He frowned. "Let's get back to work."

Wow, couldn't he be happy for me? And why did I wish they'd come from Calder instead?

That afternoon, I got to work with the design plans and ordering materials, but Emily called.

"Send me a picture," she said when I told her about the flowers, so I did. She reacted pretty much the same way as I had. "That's a lot of flowers, Mallory. Sheesh!"

"I mean, I never expected it."

"They're from a prince! Like you always wanted. Why aren't you … emoting?"

How could I explain?

Emily gave a low chuckle. "It's that Calder guy."

"No." My *no* was so weak, it was like Kool-Aid when you forget to add the sugar.

"You're not into Calder instead of the prince, are you? Because you do talk about him a lot."

Maybe I did. "It's because he's my only coworker right now. Or occasionally his parents."

"Back to my original question: you're not into him, are you?" Emily loved nailing things down, the no-nonsense businesswoman. "No hedging. I want to know."

"Look, the guy was engaged and broke up at Christmas three years ago." Not that I had more details than he'd given me at the bakery, but I'd gathered that much.

"Ouch. That had to hurt. Does he hate Christmas? And what about women?"

"Kind of both, and I totally empathize. Remember Dylan?"

"I didn't think you were dating Dylan at Christmas."

"We met at Christmas, but I did irrationally hate the Fourth of July holiday for a couple of years after the Dylan incident."

"Yeah, I remember." Emily's disgust came through the phone loud and clear. "One phone call from his ex, and poof! Gone like the smoke of a firecracker."

He'd left me—literally.

At the fireworks show.

Suddenly celebrating my personal independence.

"What I'm saying is that dating guys with complex relationship history hasn't been my thing since then." If I were honest with myself, my dating hesitation hadn't been a construction worker problem. It'd been a guys-with-issues problem.

"Good. So you're saying you can focus on Prince Reynard of the one million roses instead of the hunky history teacher."

I could try. But Calder made it pretty tough sometimes. He was just so dang great, whether or not he had issues with Christmas and dating.

Enough talking. "I gotta get back to work."

"Me, too." Emily signed off and returned to her Boston financier's whirlwind life.

"Calder?" I rounded the corner to the demolished area of what used to be the grand Hollywood Medieval Set room, hand firmly atop my hard hat. Calder had his measuring tape out. "Oh, good. You're measuring it already. What have you got for me?"

"Mahogany." He crinkled one side of his face. "Are you sure it's the right wood for this project?"

"For whatever reason, it's the prince's only stipulation." Other than looking better than the two nearby mansions.

"But we're going to paint it. The original home had all wainscoting and chair rails—all the woodwork painted."

True. And there was gold-leaf detailing, too. "Yeah, I know. Painting over the grain and color of mahogany seems like a crime. But, heh-heh. If you're a prince, you can afford to be a decorating criminal."

From Calder's dead face, my joke fell like a lead balloon.

"Sorry. What did I say wrong?"

Calder went back to measuring. "Nothing. Hey, let's choose paint colors soon."

"I have a few sample chips." Having someone along to consult always helped me with moments of indecision. I dug the samples out of the duffel I was now carrying everywhere and laid them out on the flat area of the table saw. "Do you like Snowfield and Ecru?" I held two chips side by side and studied them.

"I'm more drawn to Porcelain Bisque." He picked up a color card and stared at it. Then, he peered at the side of my face, and then at the sample again. "This ... huh." He held the card up, touching it to my cheek. "It's exactly the same."

Tingles rolled down my neck as his curled finger brushed against my skin.

I swatted it away. "Hey. We're painting a grand hall here, not my face."

"It's the exact match to your makeup."

"Hey. This isn't painted." I patted my cheeks. "Makeup makes me break out."

"You're not wearing makeup?" Calder handed me back the card. "I don't believe it."

I shoved it in my purse. "It takes a dutiful, almost *religious* avoidance of the sun to be this pale, thank you very much." I made vampire teeth at him. "Why, are you going to tease me about my wanting to suck your blood?" That had been a constant when I was a kid. I lifted my fingers menacingly and aimed for his neck.

In a surprise move, Calder tugged his t-shirt collar away and held his jugular out for me. "I succumb to the darkness."

Wow, that guy sported a serious tough-guy neck, thick and manly. I hadn't noticed it before. And the way he tugged at his t-shirt, some of the corded muscles along the tops of his shoulder peeked out.

"Heh-heh." My claws retracted and I pulled back, my sheepish laugh not covering any of my embarrassment at my own blatant desire for him. Betcha anything my face wasn't porcelain bisque at that moment. "We'll just order Porcelain Bisque with Marshmallow World for the trim. Okay? Okay."

I jumble-stepped backward, tripping over the leg of a ladder. *Whoa.* I began slow-motion falling toward the floor.

Calder shot forward—and caught me! Right around the small of my back, his strong arm capturing my waist and keeping me from hitting the ground.

Our gazes met, and I don't know if they were visible to anyone but me, but I am pretty sure rays of twinkling stars beamed between my eyes and Calder Kimball's.

"You fell." His voice was throaty, full of gravel.

"You caught me," I whispered.

We hung suspended there for who knows how many swings of the Kit-Cat clock's tail, maybe a million, while I soaked up all the delicious chemistry surging between us, steeping my very cells in it.

"Are you all right?" His gaze was soft, almost in a light-filtered haze.

"Uh-huh." In my adrenaline rush, I had become the world's most brilliant conversationalist.

Slowly, he righted me, placing me back on my feet. "Walk forward not backward, okay?"

"Okay." I planted the soles of my shoes on the floor, and then stomped them to prove I was on solid ground. "All set, *terra firma.*"

"*Carpe spero.*" Seize hope. He lifted a knowing brow—he'd seized me. Better, the guy knew his Latin phrases. Why was that such a turn-on? Maybe because I was already buzzing with his presence and touch. Add to those appeals a mind that had studied, and I was a goner.

"*Fortes Fortuna adiuvat*"—fortune favors the brave—I said, with a hint of flirtation.

Maybe I should muster some courage and show him I was getting interested. Really interested—and have the courage to forget my fading dream of a prince. My eyes were locked with Calder's, and something was passing between us in a language even more ancient than the Roman Empire's Latin.

"What's that language you're speaking?" Rochelle came sauntering through with a sledgehammer on her shoulder. "Don't tell me you're practicing Pig Latin."

"Uh-huh." My conversational skills stayed at a record high. Our gazes turned to Calder's mom, and the connection broke. "Sorry. What?"

We stepped away from each other. I put my hands in my back pockets.

"We're done in the kitchen, and I want to talk to you inside, Mallory, about adjusting the size of the room. The original home's kitchen was very small."

I followed Rochelle, but I glanced back over my shoulder at Calder as I left—risking another trip-and-fall. *But he'd catch me. I know it.*

Every time I glanced back, Calder was still watching me. The guy was a million surprises. He was one of those nesting dolls, and I kept opening and opening him up. Someday I might get to his solid core. It would be beautiful.

Maybe more beautiful and noble than even a prince's deep center.

Rochelle pattered on about kitchen remodel plans, updates, throwbacks to original design, and I registered most of it, but the bulk of my thoughts still centered on Calder Kimball.

"Hey, Rochelle?" I ventured when she paused to breathe. "Is Calder's ex-girlfriend still around?" If she was, I wanted to kick her in the shin. I wanted to tell her to leave him alone forever. I wanted to threaten to sue her.

"What insight you have, Mallory. You're the most insightful person I could have hired for this job."

"What? Why?"

"Just this morning, Darren and I were talking about Alanis. Curious, I looked her up online to find her address. She's living not far from here, actually! How insightful of you to notice that Calder seems open to the idea of a relationship again. Maybe because it's Christmas. They say it's that time of year when the world falls in love."

Uh, did Rochelle know nothing about her son's feelings? The last person he'd want to be in touch with was … was it Alanis?

Rochelle sighed. "Calder is at his worst around the holidays."

Humph. At least his mom had noted that much.

"I haven't reached out yet. But if Alanis happens to be unattached, I'd love if she'd reconsider the breakup."

Wait a minute. Alanis had been the one who'd broken up? Somehow, I'd imagined it the other way around. Calder had hinted that way, right?

"That girl ticked every box on his wife wish-list. Smart, beautiful,

64

brunette. He does love a brunette. Hey, you're a brunette. Anyway, what do you think? Should I try to get in touch with her?"

Rochelle couldn't be serious. "Um."

"You could help me plan a dinner party and we could surprise him with Alanis." She beamed like she'd solved all the problems of the universe.

I wince-beamed back. "I don't—" I coughed while I hunted for the right response.

Rochelle took an emergency call. She gave me a smile and hurried outside where the cell reception was better.

My mouth gawped like a fish's, blub-blub, as I replayed the conversation.

Had Calder broken up with Alanis like he'd implied, or had Alanis done the breaking up? To hear Rochelle, Alanis had left Calder. But why would she? Well, other than Calder did have his moody moments—but I suspect the breakup had been the catalyst for those. He could heal and be his better self, I was sure. Where did the truth lie?

Chapter 12

Mallory

"Hey, are we going to the paint store, or what?" Calder's ball-cap was at a jaunty angle. He looked like a kid with a new bicycle, refreshed. Happy. The spell of that trip-and-catch must've still held some power over him an hour later. His eyes took a slow journey from my hairline down to my toes and back. I glanced down. Oh, great. My blouse had come unbuttoned one level too low.

I grabbed at it and remedied the gape.

He was still looking into my eyes. "You have really great hair, you know that?" He picked up a lock and dropped it. "It shines."

Well, that was because I put a shine product on it every morning in hopes that Prince Reynard would notice me if he showed up. Instead, I'd gotten noticed—but not by the prince.

Calder's attention gratified me—maybe even more than if Prince Reynard had commented on it. I got the sense Calder was more sparing in his compliments than the prince was.

"Calder ..." I needed to say something to him. I wasn't sure what. I wanted to know if he'd dropped Alanis. I wanted to know if he was ready to be open to a relationship, like his mom seemed to think. But was I ready for that conversation? Had I ousted my lifelong wish to be with a prince so quickly, even as an actual prince was at my gates?

"You're not going to believe this." Rochelle bustled in. "Come and look."

The timing of this woman! My question died on my lips, unasked.

We followed Rochelle into one of the main floor bathrooms. "Will you look at that?" From the base of the shower, she yanked a couple of boxes, and then indicated for us to peer over the edge.

"Is that daylight?" I might have also seen the dirt of the ground.

"Indeed it is."

"There's no bottom in the shower?"

"Not in any of them." Rochelle chucked the debris back in. "All of the main floor showers are floorless."

"What is the point of that?" I asked.

Closing his eyes, Calder touched the side of his head, like he was a fortune teller. "I conjure the ghost of homeowners past. Tell me ghost, what do you see?" He waited, nodded, and then his eyes popped open and he dropped his hand. "DIY gone wrong."

It was the only thing that made sense. "So, what are you going to do?" I'd only worried about historical details, not shower pans, in the past. Décor, not functionality.

"It's all right. We were going to pull it anyway." Rochelle patted Calder's arm. "I just like to let him play Calder the Magnifico now and then. He's been doing it since he was about ten."

"Mom." Calder bumped her with his shoulder. "Mallory didn't need to know that."

"Oh, but I did." I grinned. "Do you hire out for bar mitzvahs?"

"My rate is far beyond what you'd like to pay, trust me." He led me out of the room, and Rochelle said she was leaving to pick up lunch for the crew and to order new shower pans.

67

We headed out to his truck to make our trip to the paint store.

"It's cool how your mom took that whole disaster in stride." At the shop, I made a last check of the color strips. Marshmallow World and Porcelain Bisque were still feeling right.

"She's used to it. In their business, it's almost something you expect every single day."

"I wish my parents had been like that." I chose a high-quality semi-gloss five-gallon bucket for the paint counter attendant to mix.

"Had been like what?" he asked while we walked down some empty aisles, away from the loud shaking of the paint mixer.

"Resilient." There was no other word for Calder's parents than that. They bounced back after major setbacks. Unlike mine.

"Well, construction is boom and bust. You just try to enjoy the boom times and save up against the next bust. A bust is always coming. You get used to it." Calder sounded used to it. I'd almost become that way myself, thanks to life's storms. "Where are your parents, anyway?"

The unspoken, *and why didn't they feed you when you were a kid* hung in the air. I probably shouldn't have told him about my grinding poverty in my youth. It clearly hurt his soul. *He cares.*

"They're ... well, I don't know where Dad is. He left after some really bad stuff happened to them financially. Then, Mom didn't rebound. She kind of let herself waste away."

Calder grabbed the shelf stacked with shellac cans. "She what?"

"Um, she died." To put it bluntly. "When I was ten. Dad left us with a massive debt that he unintentionally racked up by investing in the wrong friend's company, using up all their savings and then borrowing to double down when the friend asked. The friend then skipped town and went, I think, to a Caribbean island. According to what few documents I could find, the so-called friend put Dad's name on all kinds of promissory notes, which my trusting dad signed. It was bad. Seven figures bad. Dad was a high school basketball coach and in summertime had a lawn-care business for the neighborhood for a side income. It was way out of his ability to repay. I might have run away, too."

Calder lowered his voice and stepped up beside me. "No, Mallory. You wouldn't have."

"I—" I couldn't have. He was right.

We stood in the paint aisle. A warm light haloed Calder, and as I looked, a future painted itself between us—broad strokes, sweeping lines, pastels and bold and beautiful.

With a gentle hand, Calder moved a lock of my hair from my face to behind my shoulder. "You fended for yourself, when there was no one to protect you. You're a pretty amazing person, Mallory."

His touch was electrifying. My ears pounded with his nearness. My heart was skipping all around like a five-year-old at recess. "I'm ... just me."

"Just you is more than enough." He stepped forward, closing the space between us. A confidence and compassion in his eye mingled with desire. My lips parted, and his breath feathered against them. A kiss balanced on his mouth, ready to leap.

I was all tremors, from fingertips to belly to knees. I shouldn't kiss Calder. Not if I was going to belong to Prince Reynard. If I was going to be a princess who never had to worry about her next meal again for the rest of her born days, I couldn't go kissing even the most beautiful of coworkers.

Oh, but Calder *was* beautiful. Especially in this light, with his strong features and dark, brooding eyes. Kissing him could alter my plans, could alter everything. I ached for his kiss, his touch, his approval, his protection.

Protection. Safety.

No. I had plans. I needed to stick to my plans. They were so close to becoming mine. My phone chimed a text, as if it was an alarm clock in the morning after too nice of a dream.

I looked away, tugging at the collar points of my blouse. "We should go choose some paint, okay?" I backed up, and the small of my back caught a shelf. "I—yeah." I cleared my throat.

"Uh, right." He stepped back, releasing me from whatever power he'd had over me. "We're here to buy paint."

"Paint." I had to think about paint. Instead of the guy who spoke Latin, and who had a cheesy magic act that he was famous for in his family. And who could create a flawless length of mitered baseboard or crown molding in record time.

I grabbed for my phone. The text was from Prince Reynard! He'd texted me with a question about the design. Oh, good. I could thank him for the roses.

But I could barely read the screen. The words swam before my eyes.

Oh, no. It's happening. I'm falling for Calder Kimball.

Chapter 13

Calder

L uckily, I got caught up in a side project and couldn't paint with Mallory after all. The shower pans all had to be replaced, stat.

Compound what happened in the paint store with what had gone on between us when she fell and nearly landed on her backside in that pile of rusty nails, and I had a rough time falling asleep that night.

Toss, turn, groan, push aside the curtains and see whether Mallory's light was still on in her cottage.

It was off. She probably slept like a babe. I wasn't affecting her, obviously. At least not like she was affecting me. The arrow of Cupid, love god of Roman myth, had struck me square in the … well, let's just say he'd struck.

A guy had needs. I couldn't go the rest of my life and never be interested in another woman. When I'd sworn off dating after Alanis, had I committed to the monastic life?

Even monks historically had their weaknesses.

It would appear that Mallory Jameson was my weakness.

What if I pushed Mallory for progress? Just ask her to see where things between us went? I'd been a pretty confident dater all my life up until Alanis. Letting one bad experience preclude all other potentially good experiences was weak.

But no question, Mallory was fighting it. Fighting what I could obviously see was a great thing about to happen between us.

I chuckled and yanked at my hair. Cupid is sometimes pictured wearing armor like that of Mars, god of war. Love and war have always been closely linked.

My eyes squeezed shut. Behind them, Mallory's long waves of chestnut hair gleamed. It stretched on for miles. I luxuriated in it. After touching it today, I knew, too—that it was as soft as silk, just like it looked.

Maybe everything about Mallory was just as good as it looked.

***

The next day, I was thinking about that hair once again. Mmm.

"Dude. Watch it!" One of the construction crew—Fiske—threw a little wood chip at me, hitting my hardhat. "You're using power equipment. No daydreaming about that little brunette hottie you can't keep your eyes off. She's smokin', though. Can't say as I blame you."

My hackles rose. "You keep your eyes off her. She's out of your league." And mine, possibly. At least by measure of personal character.

However, not by social status or financial status. If I were to take my position on the company board of Royal Construction, I'd have the resources to more or less buy Mallory Jameson the services of a brigade of private chefs for every meal for the rest of her life.

Imagine her being hungry all those years! Orphaned! Her description of her figure as being *hard-won*—floored me. Her dad and mom had handled adversity wrong, no doubt, and Mallory had suffered, but she had grown strong.

She floored me.

Speaking of floors, "Guys, what happened when you pulled up the carpets upstairs?"

"Hardwoods." Fiske acted like this wasn't a big deal, but it was.

"Hardwoods. What condition?"

"Need sanding and staining."

Not removal, replacement? That would save us weeks! "Can you get a sanding crew going on that as soon as possible?" That was a ton of square footage to cover. "We'll clean them up and then stain them mahogany."

The prince would like that. And I could get Mallory away from him even a smidge faster.

Mallory walked up. "What are you staining mahogany?" She looked extra pretty this morning, her hair up in a ponytail, her t-shirt clinging in all the right ways. "I hope it's actual mahogany wood."

"No can do, Calder," Fiske interrupted before I could answer Mallory. "We're swamped with the plumbing and electrical. Have you seen what was in these walls? Check it out. But keep back. It's dangerous."

I tore my eyes off Mallory and moved to where Fiske had sledgehammered back the plaster of the walls.

Oh, no.

"Oh, no." Mallory voiced my thoughts. "It's not even knob and tube. It's bare wires!"

"Stay back." I placed a protective arm between her and the wall. The last thing she needed was a medical bill from being electrocuted. "They could be live wires."

Fiske touched the wires with an amperage tester. "Yep. Live wires. High voltage, like getting a kiss from a sexy design consultant." He shot a leering look at Mallory.

"I'm a historian." Mallory frowned and stalked out of the room.

My lip curled at him. Way to go, Fiske. I shot him a *grab those wires and hold on until you can't anymore, dude* look, and then I chased after her. She had headed for the grand staircase.

"Wait up." I joined her, matching her pace by taking two stairs at a time. "Don't mind him. He's a Neanderthal."

Her eyes flashed at me. "That's exactly the word I used for you when we met."

73

"Me!"

"Let's just say I have some experience with getting hit on by members of construction crews."

"Men can be pigs."

She lifted her eyes and met mine. "Not all of them."

Did she mean me? That I wasn't a jerk? Another one of Cupid's arrows struck me—deep in my chest, its tincture spreading like liquid sugar through my veins. "I hope I'm one of the good ones." I stepped closer to her, the sounds of the construction project downstairs jarring as loudly as ever, drowning out the rapid beats of my heart.

"Not you." She didn't back away this time. "You're a high school history teacher. That's classy in and of itself."

"It is." I'd better reinforce that idea. "Anything else about me that's not straight outta the Pleistocene Epoch?"

"Fishing for compliments much?"

"Humor me." I thirsted for her praise.

"Well, okay. For starters, you care about your parents' remodeling business enough to go help them out during your breaks, even though you have things you'd rather do, like read. You're amazing at your wood craftsmanship. It's impressive. You're impressive."

"Right?" I joked, but in those terms, I kind of was impressive. This woman had searched to know who I was at my core, not focusing on what I was eventually supposed to inherit, or my connection to Royal Construction.

In fact, she didn't even seem to know that Mom and Dad owned the conglomerate. She seemed to think they simply supervised the historic renovation subsidiary.

What would she think if she knew the truth? Suddenly, I wished she could know—not just the *teacher doing woodworking on holiday* me, the *everything* me. I longed to lay my heart bare, to tell her my hopes and fears. To plan a future and insert her in it. To convince her I was a young man of promise and secure her approval.

"Anything else?"

Mallory didn't hesitate. "You know Latin, you care about history and what's going on in the world, you're funny." With every new compliment, her cheeks reddened. "Best of all, you are good at catching people who trip over ladders." She bit her lips together and moistened them, killing me just a little.

"Only when the tripper is you." I couldn't take my eyes off her mouth. "I wasn't expecting you, Mallory."

"I definitely wasn't expecting you, Calder." She touched her collarbone, and her breaths were coming faster.

Her gaze threatened to swallow me whole. I submerged myself in its depths, swimming, luxuriating. I had to kiss her, I had to show her she needed me—my touch, my protection, my love.

Someone below yelled a few choice curse words. The noise threatened to spoil this otherwise perfect moment. I had to get her away from everyone else, have her all to myself.

I was going to kiss this woman.

"Come with me. There's something I want to show you." I took her hand and led her across the landing to a closed door. I unlocked it with the universal house key. "You need to see this view."

I extended my hand, and she took it. I interlaced my fingers with hers, electricity shooting from every skin cell. Holding tightly, I pulled her with me up the final narrow set of winding stairs. The higher we went, the less the rest of the house could be heard—or could hear us.

Soon, it opened up into the glass-paned walls of the cupola atop the house.

"Oh, wow. I had no idea you could access this from inside." Mallory spun, looking out each of the eight windows of the octagonal room. "The view is breathtaking—from the town to the ocean. Snow would make it even prettier."

Nothing could make Mallory prettier. Her spirit shone through her countenance: good, and kind, and unfathomably resilient. She was smart—smarter than I was—about survival through difficulties, and probably about a lot of other topics. I wanted to probe that mind, that character. She had her life together. Like me, she had issues, but unlike me, she was handling them with grace and determination. I ran away, and she faced her trials head-on.

No matter what else had happened to me in the past, this girl was tearing all those preconceptions to pieces, like chunks of old asphalt road broken up and piled in a heap. The newly laid road ahead—with her—looked smooth, shiny with fresh asphalt and brightly painted lines, with a road sign arrow that pointed clearly: *Happiness This Way*.

"No, I was definitely not expecting you, Mallory." I stepped toward her, and she backed up against a window. I came closer, and she tilted her chin upward, her lips parting in what I knew was an invitation—whether she meant it consciously or not.

Every view faded but her pretty, porcelain bisque face. Even the birds outside muffled into silence. All that remained was Mallory—and my need to kiss her.

She took her lower lip between her teeth. "You brought me here to show me something?" Her gaze was fixed on my mouth.

"This." I reached a hand around her waist, and another I placed at the nape of her soft neck. She tilted her chin slightly upward, and her lips parted more, showing a hint of her tongue.

I caught fire.

But I held it to a small conflagration—at first. I let my lips brush hers lightly, enough to send tingles through my every cell. I tasted her mouth, its cinnamon spice an aphrodisiac like those sought after for millennia.

"Calder." She pressed her mouth to mine, and we were kissing—two creatures made as one. It was like finding a buried treasure that I'd been unwittingly searching for on a map all my life, and she was the giant X that marked the spot for all the riches I'd ever dreamed of. Mallory was my treasure, my balm, my lighthouse.

After a luxuriantly long time, she broke away. "Silly me, I kind of thought you'd brought me up here to look at the cliffs and the ocean."

"You're a vast ocean, Mallory. I can't believe I found you."

"I—" A few clouds passed over her face, but she cleared them, and then rose up on tiptoe and kissed me softly, sumptuously one more time. I reveled in it. I didn't want it to stop. Eventually it had to. We only had six weeks on this project, and three were gone already.

Only three weeks left with her! Could I extend them? How could they last much longer? I kissed her some more while I planned, but my thoughts were a cloud bank.

Mallory's kiss obscured everything else.

When I shifted into a higher gear, she giggled and pushed me back. "We should go discuss what you think you're staining mahogany."

Letting her go—with true reluctance—I bent down and pulled at a ripped edge of the carpet. "Hardwoods under here."

"Oh, wow. Parquet, even. Up this high in the house, too." She bent to examine it. As she caressed the still-shiny surface, she educated me on a few facts of the period. "When this mansion was built, an influential designer named Eastlake was a proponent of area rugs placed on hardwoods. He said it was better for health. Rugs could be tacked down and then taken up and beaten to get the dirt out. That's why the parquet is at the perimeter here, and not in the middle." She pulled the carpet back a little farther to prove her point.

Sure enough. Parquet inlaid only at the edges. "You do know your stuff."

She looked so pretty with her hair slightly mussed, and her lips a little redder. I could stand for a repeat of today's hike to the cupola several times a day.

"I'd like to refinish these, if we can, and then search out some great area rugs that would be period appropriate."

Excellent. "Then maybe we can meet back here to discuss what else might be appropriate. I have a broad definition, just so you know."

A twinkle lit her eye. "I don't doubt it." She slipped down the stairs, and I continued pulling up the carpet like the Hulk, ripping it like it was tissue paper and not woven for strength and durability. My adrenaline might never subside.

I'd kissed that Mallory person—the most impressive woman of my acquaintance, as those historical heroes often said.

Even more significant, I'd kissed her at Christmastime—and I hadn't turned to ash and blown away like I'd expected.

The woman clearly didn't want me for my money. I couldn't help loving the fact that I'd been the one to make all of the moves on her, not the other way around. It was more than refreshing—it was brand new.

To her, I was just Calder Kimball, son of Rochelle and Darren Kimball, history teacher who also liked woodworking and used his breaks to help his family.

She seemed genuinely interested in me—for myself. Not my money or my future spot as CEO of the largest construction conglomerate on the East Coast. In fact, she almost seemed to be falling for me against her will.

Mallory was a revelation. A completely different woman from any I'd ever encountered.

Honestly, I hadn't thought of Alanis once in the past few days. Uh, there wasn't room for her anymore in my brain. Mallory took up way too much real estate.

I was falling for her, regardless of the holiday or the time of year.

On the other hand, my feelings might make me the modern Prometheus: someone who liked playing with fire—since she was obviously also interested in Prince Reynard.

I was doing my letter-best to keep him off her mind. Today, my efforts had worked like a Trojan horse, infiltrating all her defenses, and taking her down behind enemy lines.

I'd captured her.

Or, at least I'd let her capture me.

My arms loaded down with the carpet debris, I descended all the staircases. Outside, I chucked them in the roll-off, alongside all the other rotted out relics of the badness of the house. Among the bird sounds, I heard a feminine laugh. Mallory's. It was music better than the birds' songs, and I jogged around the side of the house between the kitchen door and the pool house.

"What's funny?" I came up beside her.

Mallory looked alarmed to see me. She shoved her phone into her pocket. "Calder."

"What's going on? You texting your friend Emily? I didn't figure you for the kiss and tell type." I went in for another kiss, but she dodged me.

She hadn't been texting Emily. Obviously.

"I asked the prince about the area rug idea. He said it was great with him."

He'd clearly said more—including something amusing. Her face was flushed. She walked toward her bungalow, but she shot me an apologetic glance.

No. This was not going to happen. I wouldn't allow it. The last thing that amazing woman needed was a gambling debtor. I had to stop the ball from rolling that direction.

But if kissing her like we kissed upstairs wasn't enough, what was?

Chapter 14

Mallory

Kissing Calder had been a mistake.

A delicious, elevating, soaring experience—but a wrong move nonetheless. Calder couldn't take care of me financially, not like a prince could.

I analyzed the kiss three ways from Sunday, and finally I landed on this explanation: Calder had been caught up in the moment, after our heated interludes—when I tripped, and then in the paint store when I'd told him the things I liked about him and vice versa. The chemistry had been crazy between us, and he'd simply needed to get kissing me out of his system.

It wasn't as if he'd want my kiss again. One and done.

Like I'd told him—I wasn't expecting him. Hadn't he understood what I'd meant by that? That I wasn't ready for him, or someone like him. Or with a kiss like his. Or a mind and a heart …

Oh, shoot. Did *I* understand what I meant by it?

"Lumber yard?" I asked, as Calder held the door of his old truck open for me. "I thought we were planning on refinishing, not putting down new floors throughout. And then adding rugs. I'm on the trail of some great rugs right now."

He started up the truck and headed us down the drive toward the main road. "We are, but my parents' floor sander died on their last job. They weren't expecting to use it on this one, and for whatever reason, they're back-ordered. Anderson Lumber has the only rental availability in five hundred miles. And there are none to purchase. Everything's on back-order."

"Doesn't Royal Construction have a sander we could use? And a crew of ten to loan for this job?" We had carte blanche.

"Sadly, no. Every bit of manpower is stretched with other deadlines, and the company's sanders are all being used as part of a government contract."

Oh, government.

"Have you used a hardwood sander?"

"Some. Besides, everyone agreed that you and I are tasked with all decisions and work related to the hardwood—since, as you said, the prince cares about it so much."

"Okay," I said. Why did Calder say *the prince* with a hint of venom? The guy was our paycheck.

Funny, I hadn't thought of Prince Reynard nearly as much in the past couple of days. Although, right after Calder kissed me, I'd had a sudden vision of a disappointed look on Reynard's face, like I'd let him down. More likely it was my own conscience telling me that kissing Calder could be squandering my chance with the prince—the prince with whom I was on a first-name basis. Reynard had made me laugh in that text about—

"Oh, look. It's snowing!"

"Cool. First snow of the year." Calder said this so casually—as if it wasn't momentous.

"Pull over!" I shouted. "Please? Can you just?"

"Uh, Mallory. Why are you suddenly hyperventilating?" But he pulled to the side of the wooded path that served as our road.

I jumped out and held my mitten's palm skyward. "Catch one. The first one you see."

Calder had come out of the still-running truck and stood beside me, while I ran hither and thither trying to catch a flake. They were elusive today. "Aw, come on."

None of them fell into my glove.

I whipped it off. Maybe the sky required bare skin for it to grant its blessings to me. "I'll get one. You'll see." I ran back and forth, but to no avail.

"Mallory." Calder laughed, possibly at me, not with me. "You're acting like you've contracted one of those mysterious dancing plagues of the Middle Ages. Like you're going mad."

"I'm getting madder by the minute." A second ago, there'd been thousands of flakes, and now the sky had shut itself back up again. "Do you see any more flakes? Should we drive back a few hundred yards?" I turned around and looked down the road, holding a hand up to shade my eyes. "Did we drive completely through the flurry and leave it behind?"

Calder came to my side and placed his hands on my hips, looking pointedly down into my face until I directed my attention at his regal nose and his dark hair and rugged good looks. "What are you doing?" He wore an amused smile.

"It's the first snowfall." Obviously, he hadn't been schooled in the magical properties. "If you catch a flake from the first snow, you can make a wish." On love. I didn't add that part, even though it was important.

"What kind of wish?"

Ah, he'd nailed it. "A wish on love," I said, lowering my eyes. I know my face was coloring. "You think it's dumb."

"I think it's really cute." He pressed his forehead to mine. "There's not a lot you could do I would think was cuter. Unless ..." He crooked a finger and lifted my chin, as if to kiss me again.

I forgot all about the snowflake wish, as my breath caught and I fell toward Calder's delicious—

A horn honked.

82

"I was right!" The window of a truck was rolled down, and Rochelle peered out of it. "I thought you two had been spending a lot of alone-time together."

Calder sprang back, but then he softened and placed an arm around my shoulder. "Go ahead, Mom. You know you want to congratulate yourself."

"Not me." Her eyes twinkled, the window rolled up, and the truck with the Royal Construction: Renovation Division magnet on the door drove off.

"Awesome. Caught making out with the boss's son." So much for catching snowflakes. I hustled to Calder's truck and climbed inside. "I'm so embarrassed. Like I just spilled red wine on someone's antique white carpet."

"Don't be." We got back in the truck, and Calder moved us back onto the road. "She's probably back at Buckworth Castle now, texting her sister with glee."

I didn't really want to be the subject of gleeful texts. Rochelle shouldn't be matchmaking me with Calder—wasn't it kind of unethical? Or was I the one with the murky ethics here? Just a few days ago, Rochelle had told me she wanted Calder back together with Alanis. I doubted she'd changed her focus.

Me? I was just a way for Calder to get back on his feet. A stepping stone back to Alanis, back toward opening his heart to the possibility of love. Not the intended destination, for sure.

Just like with Dylan—every guy was waiting for his ex to pop back into the picture.

Three twists down the road, though, a different car passed.

Prince Reynard's.

Instinct made my knees pull up to my chest. I threw my arms around them, hugging them tight. One minute or so earlier, and the prince would have seen me kissing Calder in the first snowfall.

I needed to really consider what I was doing—and what I should be doing.

Chapter 15

Calder

With the precious rental sander in tow, we lugged it up the several flights of stairs. "It's better to start at the top," I said. "Then we can sweep all the sawdust downward as we go."

"Let gravity do some of the work. I like it." Mallory placed a white cone mask over her mouth and nose and put on her safety goggles. She looked really cute in them. The way the tool belt sat, slung around her hips, it was all I could do to not go over and take her by the waist and pull her to me, every curve of her pressing against my torso, and …

We had to finish this job, or else I was going to be late returning to St. Dominic's.

"Don't forget what the guy at the rental counter said." Mallory pulled on her work gloves.

"That it's a two-person job, not a one-person job?" I didn't need much convincing to be glad to work with her—hand-in-glove, as Mom had said. We were actually turning into a pretty good team, in a lot of unexpected ways.

"No, the other thing."

"To hold on tight?" I'd absolutely be thinking of holding on tight.

"Got it."

She bent down and plugged it in. Luckily, the wiring had already been redone on this, the cupola floor, and in all the second floor rooms as well. Only the main floor was a horrific fire code violation.

"Ready?" Her finger was poised over the start switch, and I nodded. "Hi-ho, Silver. Away!"

She flipped it, and the machine lurched forward across the wood floor, nearly yanking my shoulders out of their sockets. "Whoa, there, Silver." With my full strength, I was able to pull it back into submission.

"That was scary," Mallory yelled. "I'm getting out of the way." She stepped behind me and picked up a stray nail we'd overlooked when sweeping.

It took all my wits and muscle to wrangle the Electric Sander with a Mind of its Own, but an hour later, we had finished our first area. The cupola's parquet floors went well!

Next, we did the tops of the descending stairs to the floor below. The edges would have to be done with a handheld sander.

I was sweating by the time we reached the second floor.

"Eleven rooms on this floor," she said, after a jog down the hall to count the doors. "We're on a roll. We'll be on the main floor in no time."

If by *no time* she meant five and a half hours, she was exactly right. We managed the grand staircase next, and ended up on the main floor, dusty and physically spent.

"It's getting hot." I switched it off and felt the metal over the motor. "Should we let it rest?" And take some time for ourselves? "The fog has burned off by now. Want to go up and look out at the ocean in the cupola again?"

"Oh, was it foggy last time?" She had a cute giggle. "I'm afraid I didn't notice."

Oh, yeah. That's what I liked to hear. I'd distracted her entire attention with my engrossing kisses. In a few seconds, I'd be doing that again.

As we climbed back up the stairs, Mom came down them, blocking our path. "What are you two doing?"

"What are you doing?" I asked. Then I saw the window cleaner in her hands.

"How's the floor-sanding project going?" Mom continued toward us, and we had no option but to back down, since the stair was too narrow for passage. "I got a call from the store. They have another customer who reserved it for Thursday at ten, and they'd forgotten to check. They'll need it back by then."

Drat. No time to rest. Even to make out.

"Silver seemed hot. We didn't want it to overheat." My excuse sounded weak.

"Silver?"

"That's the brand name of the sander," Mallory explained.

"Huh. Well, I'm pretty sure the two of you know all about overheating." Mom gave a wicked laugh. Curse her. "Bye, now. Don't waste time during working hours. We'll be dining with Prince Reynard tonight, and I'd like to be able to report significant progress."

Right. The prince.

Mom left, but Mallory had gone pale. Even paler than her usual porcelain tone.

"Are you okay?" I headed back toward the room where we'd left the sander. "Don't worry about Mom. She teases, but she's harmless."

Mallory shook her head. "Let's just keep going so we can give a good report."

"Aye-aye, captain." We maneuvered the sander to the grand hall with its floor-to-ceiling windows. We'd aim to complete as many other rooms on this floor as we could finish tonight. I grabbed hold of the sander with a firm grip. "Switch it on. I'm ready."

We finished half of the grand hall, which was enormous. It was almost nightfall—which came early this time of year in Rhode Island. My shoulders were killing me. I shrugged them and rotated my left shoulder to shake out the tightness.

Mallory saw me and came over behind me. "Let me." She laid hands on my shoulder, gently massaging away the tension. "It's getting knotted right here. I can feel it."

"That's exactly where." My eyes closed, and I soaked in the healing of her touch. "Yep, right there. Ah." I exhaled heavily. She knew just how to release that tension and pain. "You're good at this."

"You should have let me run the sander."

"Silver would have bucked you off, Kimosabe."

"I'm stronger than I look." She left the first shoulder and moved to the other. Her touch was magical healing waters.

"So was our Silver. Lots stronger." I exhaled.

"Who's stronger?" In walked Fiske, strutting, eyeing Mallory like she'd be falling at his steel-toed boots any second. "Pretty sure I can bench more than anyone else on the crew."

"The sander is the strongest." Mallory's massage increased in power, but I didn't react. Not aloud, anyway. "Stay back from it."

The sander lay atop the sand-colored sawdust like a sphinx in the desert, or more likely, a cat ready to pounce.

Fiske scoffed. "Oh, please. If Calder can do it, so can I." He bent over to plug it back in. "Watch."

"No, Fiske. Seriously, it's—" But I wasn't fast enough. He'd flipped the on-switch with his foot even before grabbing the handles.

With a screaming whir of its motor, Silver shot forward—straight across the floor, and *right through the floor-to-ceiling plate glass window.*

Into the back yard.

Where there were some spiky juniper shrubs getting the sand knocked out of them.

Luckily, it yanked its plug out of the socket on its way, and now just lay as a dying-motor wind-down emanated from its innards.

"Oh, my gracious!" Mallory raced to the wall and leaned out of what remained of the window. "I'm so glad it didn't hit anyone."

"Don't fall through." I joined her, pulling her a step back, making sure neither of us stepped on any shards. "Are you all right?"

She nodded. She looked flushed. I should mention, Mallory was even prettier when flushed.

"Golly!" Fiske said but used a different word. Then he took off his ball cap and ruffled his hair. "You gotta warn a guy. That thing was feral."

Idiot. "Go pick it up and check it for damage, Fiske." *And quit trying to impress Mallory with your not-so-greatness. It won't work.* Besides, she was belonging to me more and more with every passing day. For once, I was loving my Christmas break. "Then bring it back inside or take it to my dad." Dad could repair anything.

"Yeah, all right." He was practically glum. As he left, Fiske shot Mallory a look that said, *it's better to have loved and lost.* Or something a lot cruder but with the same intent.

"I hope it still works." Mallory grimaced and wisely dragged a piece of four-by-eight plywood to cover the hole in the glass. I helped. "We still have this whole level to finish, and someone else needs it when we're done."

"If not, we'll drive as far as Atlanta to buy a different one, if we have to." And maybe she'd sit right by me in the truck. I'd clear a spot. "That wouldn't be so bad. We'll figure it out. It's doable."

"It'd waste precious hours of Prince Reynard's time."

The prince. I really should tell Mallory what I'd overheard. "About him," I began, and then cleared my throat because it frogged up. She did need to know.

"What about him?" Her chin turned toward me, and I took a steadying breath.

If I told her, she'd react one of several ways—possibly rejecting the truth and blaming me for meddling. Still, I couldn't *not* tell her. That would be worse. "Mallory, he's probably not the guy that you—"

In barged Dad. "What just happened in here?" He pointed at the window. "Plate glass. That one was period-specific. Replacement costs a fortune and takes a long time to ship."

That was not good. But worse was the fact Dad had interrupted what I needed to tell Mallory.

Mallory piped up, "The prince said carte blanche. We'll get it ordered immediately. Let's take measurements."

The phrase carte blanche made me wince. Carte blanche on what money?

Not my problem, but I also hated the idea of knowing people were likely to default on loans. Mallory would hate it even more. I needed to tell her.

"The sander is kaput, too." Dad growled some kind of a curse. "It'll take me all night to repair it. The store needs it back. It's their only sander. They have other people lined up to rent it. I don't want a bad reputation locally for being a rental tool destroyer."

Much as I ought to rat out Fiske for the foolhardy accident, I didn't. Luckily, Dad didn't point the finger of blame directly at me or at Mallory.

"We'll be more careful. I promise," I said, sounding contrite.

"I'll work on repairing this one, but you get another one rented in Providence in the meantime."

When Dad left, Mallory winced up at me. "That was so bad."

"Nah. He's mad, but he gets over things." Unlike her dad, apparently. "Besides, if we drive to Providence, maybe we'll see another first snow."

"Oh, well, a second first snow is actually just a second snow. It won't count." She sounded glum.

"There are hard and fast rules to this wishing thing?" I steered her aside, to an alcove. "Is it like with birthday candles—if you tell your wish, it won't come true? Or like the Trevi Fountain in Rome, where you have to toss a coin with your right hand over your left shoulder with your back to the fountain, and then you'll return to the Eternal City soon?"

"Something like that."

89

"So, who taught you about this wish tradition?"

"My best friend Emily. She heard it from her grandma."

"Emily, huh? How old were you at the time?"

"Sixteen. We were at Emily's family cabin. Jayne, Emily, and me. It was a fun holiday."

That struck a chord for me—someone named Jayne at a cabin. But it couldn't be the same person I'd met last year. Too slim of a chance. "So, sixteen-year-olds. What do they wish for? Wait." I knew this one. I did teach high school, after all. "I remember now. They wish on love. Twue wuv." I used the speech-impediment-laced voice from the marriage officiator in that movie about the princess.

"And mawwiage, if you must know." She crossed her arms over her chest. "Come on. It's probably time for dinner. Let's go."

Oh, no. She wasn't getting off that easily. I caught her elbow and eased her back before she could head out to the pool house. "Is another rule that the first time you wish on the first snow it's more powerful than the other times?" I stepped closer, taking her in my arms. She dipped her chin, but I lifted her face so she'd look up into mine. "I can see that it is."

"That's what my friend's grandma said."

"Grandmas know these things." Originators got to make the rules. "Now, the sixty-four thousand dollar question."

"Don't ask it, Calder. Don't."

Oh, but I had her right where I wanted her. "What did you wish for, on that long-ago winter night, with a snow crystal melting in your palm? Did he have an aquiline nose? Was he a brilliant historian and teacher—and even more brilliant with his hands?" I brushed a caress down her neck. "I mean his woodworking hands' brilliance, of course. And did he have a penchant for strong-hearted brunettes with doe-eyes? Tell me."

Her chin wobbled. "I—it's not important. It was a long time ago."

The more she protested, the more I needed to know. "You've been truthful with me thus far, haven't you?"

She nodded. Her eyes dropped. "Yes."

"Then, tell me." Why I was being so persistent I had no idea. But if she'd wished for me, or for a guy like me, then I guess a little part of me wanted to count it as supernatural intervention in our lives. Fate, destiny.

Or a kind and gracious God who'd heard the secret prayer of a young woman for whom life had been more than unfair.

"I wished"—she gulped—"for someone royal."

"Royal." My middle name. My mom's maiden name. The name of my grandparents' company. "Is that right?" Hope sparked a thousand firefly-sized lights in me.

"For a prince."

Oh.

I released her. It was time to go to dinner.

Chapter 16

Mallory

E ven the most delicious Cobb salad of my life didn't have much flavor tonight. Not even bacon lightened my mood.

"Miss Jameson is not as impressed with tonight's meal, I see." Prince Reynard sent me a pointed look. "Perhaps you need to fire your chef. Or tonight you have a secret substitute in your kitchen. She has a discerning palate that is not pleased."

"No, no!" I ate a forkful, but it grew in my mouth and took forever to chew, and even longer to swallow. "It's fine," I said through the remaining mouthful.

No one was convinced.

"Are you under the weather?" Rochelle refilled my water glass. "You might have inhaled too much sawdust today, especially if your mask wasn't fitted tightly enough."

"That could be it." It was much easier to agree than to explain. "I think I'll just head back to my bungalow."

"Good night, sweet Miss Jameson." Prince Reynard pushed his chair back and partially stood when I stood to leave. Such good manners. So refined.

"We'll give a tour to show the prince the house's progress so far."

Calder's dad walked me to the door. "You just take care of getting better. We'll need you tomorrow as we start the baseboards and crown molding."

Right. With Calder. Whose eyes had burned pure fury at my admission from an hour ago, leaving my insides singed.

Was there aloe vera for internal burns?

Back in my bungalow, I lay on my back and called Emily.

"It's about time you updated me!" She was breathing hard, probably working on some kind of corporate investment's details while running on the treadmill. The overachiever never rested. "I've been dying to know."

"Do you have time for a long story?"

"For you, all the time in the world. Well, until my meeting tomorrow morning at five."

"Five!"

"It's with the London office."

Made sense. I should start at the beginning. "Do you remember when we went with Jayne to your grandparents' cabin on that snowy night?"

"Sure—and we wished on the first snowfall." Emily still had all the details at her disposal: how Jayne had wished for a guy just like our hunky high school English teacher to sweep her off her feet, and that Emily had wished for someone to both kiss *and* propose to her on a bridge. "And you were the most ambitious of us all with your aim for a prince. Not that I can blame you. Princes William and Harry were still available back then, and they did look kinda tempting at the time."

Seemed like forever ago. "Then you can see how the snowflakes somehow got their wires crossed about my wish and Jayne's."

"I thought Calder teaches history, not English."

"Not the point."

"Ohhh." There was some beeping, and it sounded like the footfalls slowed. "You're saying the prince is not in the picture but the teacher is?"

"Was."

"You're not making sense."

I knew that. I slowed down and told her everything—ending with my True Confession about the original first-snowfall wish.

"You didn't!" Emily gave an appropriate-level-of-horrified gasp. "Why did you feel the need to tell him? He didn't need to know. It wasn't any of his business."

"For whatever reason, my gut requires me to be completely truthful with him. He's been burned by a liar before. I can't do that to him."

"Not even on a cruel-to-be-kind basis? Telling the truth doesn't necessarily mean telling everything you know."

"Spoken like a true businesswoman, queen of mergers and investments."

"Hey, I always let investors know there are risks."

"Look, the thing is, that for a split second, when I first said I'd wished to marry royalty, he seemed kind of happy. But then, when I was clearer, he pretty much breathed fire on me. Dragon-level heat. Melt my eyebrows off." I felt for my eyebrows. "But I've kissed him."

Emily dragged out a sigh. "Girl, I told you to keep your distance from the construction workers and only have eyes for the prize. The prize being the prince. You of all people are someone I believe can stay focused on a worthy goal."

"I—I got sidetracked." By his dark brow and his muscular neck and shoulders, and how they'd felt under my hands just the other day. So delicious. "And he's super smart. When I'm around him, I feel like I can tell him everything."

"Seems like you can't *not* tell him anything."

True. But he made me feel safe. Secure. Emotionally and intellectually. There was something to be said for that, even if he wasn't as rich as a prince.

"But can he kiss?" Emily had a knack for bringing things back to their simplest terms.

"Believe me—the guy kisses like he's been in the Olympics kissing competition and won the gold medal for the past decade."

"You're in a lot of trouble." Emily was great at stating the obvious. "I guess you have to ask yourself—what do you really want, at your deepest core."

At the center of my Russian nesting dolls?

Easy, I never wanted to be hungry or worry about finances again as long as I lived. I couldn't really tell Emily that. She'd had no idea growing up that the reason I often blew off her and Jayne about hanging out on weeknights and weekends was because I was working two or three jobs. "What I need most is security."

"Then, which of the current paths you can choose is most likely to provide that? Choose it and work toward it with the single-minded fervor that we all love and admire in our friend Mallory Jameson."

She made it sound so simple.

But it wasn't. Unless I could just figure out which of the two men was most likely to offer me that security—and whether financial security was the biggest kind of security my soul still craved.

Because Calder was filling all my other security needs, and that felt pretty right. And he was incredibly attractive, beyond my wildest expectations. That fact might be obscuring my judgment about everything else.

I was in trouble. My goals were in trouble. Or maybe they were just changing—from being protected by a prince's financial coffers to belonging to Calder.

His look of disdain when I mentioned the prince as my snowfall wish flashed into my memory. He might not want me anymore after what I'd said.

Chapter 17

Calder

I shut out all the awkwardness that plagued me. Whether I liked the fact that Mallory was into that leech of a prince or not, the project still had to be completed.

And then I was going back to St. Dominic's.

It didn't hold as much appeal for me.

Should I just tell her who I am?

But if she rejected the Calder Royal Kimball version of me …

"Measure twice, cut once." Mallory was pretty cute reciting the mantra I'd taught her. She was leaning over the stack of baseboard lengths I'd created, and we'd been measuring and doing corner cuts all morning. "Is this edge going to be mitered, too?"

"Yep, for an exterior corner."

"Convex angle, then. Got it." She used a pencil to draw the forty-five degree angle and then took the board to the table saw. There was sawdust on her t-shirt and the tops of her shoes. A little in her hair, too. Very cute.

I stifled a sigh of longing. Kisses weren't on the menu anymore.

But, merciful heavens above! A sawdust-covered woman stood beside me. I'd never dreamed how sexy that combination could be.

"You're looking at me funny." She arched a brow at me.

"Uh-huh." I came over to help steady the length of board hanging off the edge of the table. "It's a tough job, but somebody has to do it."

"You're saying I'm tough to look at?" She brushed her shirt. "Oh, man. I'm covered in this stuff." She brushed more vigorously.

"Let me help."

"Hey." She protested but with an enormous grin.

Yeah, I was totally a glutton for punishment. The woman had set her sights on that doofus of a prince.

The question still plagued me: could I change her mind with my charm, without telling her what I'd overheard about his gambling debts?

Nope. Like I'd taught myself a hundred times, people always shot the messenger. The last thing I wanted was to get shot—and ruin my shot with this amazing woman. My gut said to bide my time. Just be cool. Be the coolest guy she knew, and things would play into my favor.

My gut was driving me crazy—I itched for action, for closure—to know whether she'd see him for what he really was and choose me—or not.

Another stifling, but this time a groan instead of a sigh.

"There." She set down the board. "Do we have enough finishing nails loaded in the gun?"

"I think so. I'll check." I examined the power tool. "All set."

Mallory started humming, and it was a familiar tune but I couldn't make it out. Whether I was writhing in anguish over her preference of the prince or not, together we made a not-too-shabby work duo. Sometimes it was like she read my mind and picked up a tool or a piece of finished lumber that I needed even before I could ask for it.

Better, she seemed to have forgiven me—at least somewhat—for pushing her about her snow-wish thingie. Maybe I should apologize for that.

Or not. Probably better to let that lie.

"Sleigh bells ring," she mutter-sang.

"Oh! That's what you're humming." The Christmas song clicked into place, and filled me with emotional whiplash, as my mind filled in the blanks of the lyrics to "Winter Wonderland," the holiday love ballad.

Christmas. With a woman.

I—I didn't do that combo.

Except I am. And it's not bad.

Yeah, that was only because I was with this woman I knew wouldn't lie to me. If there was one thing recent events had taught me, it was that Mallory Jameson was no fake.

"If it would just snow a little more, we could be walkin' in a winter wonderland out along the sea-cliff coast." She bent over to pick up a stray finishing nail. "I bet it looks really pretty once the sad dirt of autumn gets covered over by snow."

"You think of dirt as sad?" I stood up and brushed off my dust-covered knees.

"Sure, especially when it's mulched with dead leaves."

"But dirt and mulch make things grow."

She altered the lyrics and sang yet a different Christmas tune. "Let it grow, let it grow, let it grow."

"Funny." I pushed the edge of some waste wood at her shoulder, just a nudge. "You're kind of cute." It just came out, I swear.

"So are you." She colored and dropped her eyes, which made her even cuter. Blast it! I had to win her over to my side! Make her forget all about that gambler, make her only have eyes for me. Every minute I was with her, I wanted her more.

"Oh, now I'm cute, am I?" I stepped closer to her, close enough to catch her cinnamon spiced scent and to want to reach for her, when—

"Who's cute?" Heavy footfalls clomped across the hardwoods and into the room.

"Prince Reynard?" Mallory straightened and patted her hair, getting it saw-dustier. "We didn't expect you today."

"I came with a purpose." His Continental accent made him sound snooty and fake. Okay, I just couldn't stand the guy.

Mallory batted her lashes at him.

I knew the look. I'd been on the receiving end of it a thousand times from every girl I met—except Mallory.

Worse, all of a sudden, the prince was exuding charisma. He was all smiles, and with his knitted beanie on, most of his less-than-GQ features were being covered up.

And if I could sense the charisma, no doubt Mallory was swimming in it.

"For what reason did you come, Prince Reynard? Not just to check on progress?"

"My parents, the king and queen, are taking a tour of the East Coast of the U.S. prior to the Christmas celebration in our country, and they will be the guests of honor at a gala given at Evergreen Point in Seacliff tomorrow night, as a kind of excuse to welcome me to the area as its newest resident." He gave a faux-humble nod of his head. "They asked me to please attend and to bring a guest."

Well, I wasn't illiterate when it came to the writing on the wall, and trust me—I wasn't letting this happen. He was not snagging my girl to be his date.

Yes, I knew how much I exaggerated.

"What a gracious and welcoming area you're moving into." I stepped right in front of Mallory, between her and the prince, effectively breaking the electric gaze passing between them. "Sure, Prince Reynard. I'd love to attend. That's so kind of you to offer. Since my parents are the architects of your future here in Seacliff, I'd love to be there as their representative and your guest."

It was small of me. Absolutely the lowest I'd ever stooped—and honestly, my first big foray into mate-guarding behavior.

But this was about Mallory's future.

"Ah, young Kimball. You'd like to attend as well? I'll see about securing you a seat at one of the other tables." His tone implied the tables that would be set up in a building ten miles away from himself and Mallory.

Humph.

"Miss Jameson." Reynard sidestepped me and reached for her hand. "Would you be so kind as to accompany me to the dinner and dancing?"

"Dancing?" Her voice was breathy.

I was going to hit the ceiling. This guy and his schmooziness and—

My phone rang. I reached for it, whipping it up to my ear. "Yeah?"

"Calder. You must feel more familiar with me than you have in the past. That's a good thing." It took a second for the voice's timbre to register for me. "I'd like us to be closer."

"Dr. Shallenberger?" The principal at St. Dominic's. My throat went dry. I'd just disrespectfully answered a call from my boss, and … oh, geez. "What can I do to help you?"

"Come to dinner with me. I'll be in Seacliff tomorrow night."

"You're what?" I stepped away from Mallory and the prince and their little theatrical performance. "Why are you in town?" And how had she known where I was? I didn't think I'd been detailed with her about my location this break.

"That sorority sister of mine I told you about mentioned your family's renovation project."

Why did that not surprise me?

"Dulcie's actually entertaining some sort of low-grade aristocrats from Europe and needs a few more couples to fill up the room." Dulcie Delacourt-Tremaine. Ah. From Evergreen Point, the palace with all the evergreens. "A lot of the movers and shakers in the village happen to be in the Caymans this time of year."

Of course they were. And there couldn't *possibly* be more than one royal family visiting Seacliff tomorrow night.

Doesn't mean I want to spend the evening with my boss, or to spend it watching the girl I was falling for be courted by … the court jester there.

100

I glanced at Mallory and Prince Reynard. He still seemed suspended, as if she hadn't given him a definite yes or no. For a brief second, her gaze strayed toward me, but the guy grabbed for her hand and pulled her attention back to him.

Mallory looked torn.

I didn't answer Dr. Shallenberger. I wouldn't until I heard Mallory's answer.

Chapter 18

Mallory

Prince Reynard clasped my fingers tightly, almost too tightly. "I need your effervescence to balance out my parents' dourness."

Dourness? That didn't sound like a fun dinner. "Are they weighted down with the cares of running a kingdom?"

"Something like that." Reynard lowered his chin, which was covered with a five o'clock shadow, his gaze probing mine. "They will be impressed with you."

With me? Ha. "I doubt that." I was no one. I'd spent a lot of my life clawing my way up dirt cliffs. Alone. There was another reason I thought dirt wasn't charming. I'd eaten a handful of it one time, just in case it had nourishment.

I glanced at Calder, helpless to know what to do. Prince Reynard was everything I'd wished for—and he'd even asked me on a date to meet his parents.

His dour parents. Wince.

But Calder … and his delightful parents …

"Wear whatever you have that's best." He gave me a nod, not actually waiting for my affirmative response, and then he was gone before I could protest.

Reynard was quoting Austen, too. My life was a movie script right now.

"Wait, Prince ..."

Calder finished up his phone call and swaggered over. "I guess you're going, huh?"

If he hadn't taken that call, if he'd kept standing between me and Prince Reynard, I would have possibly put up more of a protest against the dour dinner.

"I guess so." I couldn't muster much enthusiasm, even though on the surface I was getting everything I'd ever wanted. Maybe even more. "Reynard's a good guy. It's a pretty big honor to meet his parents."

"Just guessing, but my parents are probably more affable."

No one could describe Rochelle and Darren Kimball as *dour*. "Possibly. But they're just doing a small business, keeping it real. They don't have a nation's economy to worry about—" How many people lived in Reynard's nation, anyway? Normally, I'd be all over the details of that. I could never quite get the name of the country right and—"and tons of people's livelihoods at stake. Families." Who needed food on their tables.

"Um ..." Calder turned slightly away from me, as if to hide his expression. "Right." He collected himself and looked at me again.

"I didn't mean to offend you by saying something like your mom and dad aren't as important as Reynard's. They're great. It's just they're not a king and a queen, and ... you know what? Never mind. Let's leave it at your mom and dad are two of the best people that I've ever met, and that they've made me feel like one of their family, and I love them. A lot."

Now I was sounding like a simpering lunatic. But I did feel that way about them. And apparently I kept expressing the fact in different terms, unstoppably. "They're so solid and steady. Everything I wish my parents had been. Everything I'd like to be when I grow up."

A little tear stung my eye, but I dashed it out. Then I sniffed. Very ladylike. Totally ready to meet royalty.

"You're not grown up?" A little smile played at the side of Calder's mouth.

"No, and neither are you, so don't judge." I pushed him. "We're still kids until we're running our own businesses or married with kids of our own."

"Married. You want marriage and kids, Mallory?" Calder's eyes were sincere.

I couldn't lie to him. "I do. So much. Someday more than anything I want to create the family I always wished I'd had—one like you grew up in."

"It'll help a lot if you try to achieve that goal with someone who knows what you're talking about, and who can make family like that happen since he's been brought up in one."

Good point.

Did Prince Reynard have a family like that? He had servants. He had royal parents. Were they hands-on parents, partners in raising their son?

There was a lot I didn't know about him.

Or about life in general.

Except that I now had a date with a relative stranger to a stuffy dinner in an uncomfortable dress to meet the guy's parents.

Who were dour.

"I should be more excited."

"You should."

Had I said it aloud? "I didn't mean that. I'm so honored. What an opportunity."

"Yeah. But, hey. I guess I'll see you there."

Dude. "Calder, he didn't actually invite you." I'd seen through Calder's cute ruse, trying to protect me from unwelcome advances. Very sweet of him. "It's all right, though. Reynard knew you were joking."

"No, I know." Calder lifted the nail gun and rested it on his shoulder like it was a machine gun and he was a guerrilla warrior. "In a crazy coincidence, I was just invited to the same party by someone else. My friend Kjersten happens to be in town for it and asked if I'd be her plus-one."

Kjersten! Why were my veins suddenly full of cold pellets of lead? "Oh," was all I could manage. "I guess I'll see you there then."

Same dinner, but Calder would have a different woman on his arm.

Not me. Would she be prettier and more articulate than I am? Did Calder kiss her in a cupola every chance he got?

I should definitely not be feeling this much disappointment. "It'll be great. I brought the perfect dress."

"For a royal gala?" Calder eyed me suspiciously. "You brought something like that to a worksite? You're kidding."

"A woman always has to be prepared." And I'd known Prince Reynard would be on the scene. He was royalty. He was wealth incarnate. He'd be able to give me the safest lifestyle I could ever dream of. I'd never have to be afraid of poverty again.

Could Calder guarantee me that?

No. Even he admitted that construction was boom and bust, and that his parents had seen dire straits. With Calder's school-teaching salary, if I chose to take a chance with him, we'd likely have a lot of weeks with rice and beans for dinner. Boxed macaroni.

Or … nothing. My heart kerplunked. The cupboards could potentially be bare.

My stomach growled, muscle memory.

I grabbed at it. *I'm not going to let that happen. I don't care if Calder is better at everything else—Prince Reynard will keep me warm and fed no matter what.*

"Actually, I'm really excited to be going with the prince. He said his parents will like me." And that usually meant a young man had … intentions. Especially an aristocratic man. I knew this. I'd read novels about royalty—which might not make me an expert, but so what?

According to fiction, royal sons didn't court much, and they moved fast if they were serious about a girl. Reynard didn't seem to be toying with me or with my feelings. He was striking fast. Meeting the parents as our first date? That was lightning speed.

But I was up for it.

I was going to let Prince Reynard catch me, and I'd just have to let the idea of Calder Kimball—the history teacher with the amazing kiss and the endless list of skills and interests and similarities to me—go.

Chapter 19

Calder

I straightened the bowtie on my tuxedo.

"My son. Looking so sharp." Mom wolf-whistled.

Moms should not wolf-whistle.

"I have to look my best. It's a dinner with my boss in the presence of royalty." And oh, look. Mom was dressed up, too. "Wait a second. You're going? Is Dad?"

"Yeah, the historical society president came to me and asked if we could attend. I guess half the population of Seacliff is in Bermuda for the month." She shivered. "That means us."

She probably meant the Caymans. "I guess we'll be a big happy family there," I said.

"And I can meet your date!"

"She's my boss."

"Your boss who asked you on a *date*." She winked at me. "Is that kosher these days? For whatever reason, I got the sense no intra-school dating would be allowed."

Me, too. "That's why this isn't a date."

"Fine, fine. Besides, I've seen the way you and Mallory Jameson look at each other. I can't blame you for thinking she's special. That girl is amazing. Do you know, she could pull facts and figures out of her head for exactly which rooms in the house would need wallpaper, and which would need paint? She knows her stuff. She's a gem, Calder."

She was. And I was letting her slip through my fingers. "You know the phrase *snitches get stitches*?" I needed to warn Mom and Dad about Prince Reynard, and ask Mom's advice about whether to break the bad news to Mallory.

"Sure. Everyone does." Mom broke into a giggle. "Where did that topic come from all of a sudden?"

In walked Dad. He was in a suit—no tuxedo. "Who's making my best girl laugh?" He pecked Mom's cheek. "You look beautiful, sweetheart." Then, he turned to me. "Who's your date again, son?"

"Not a date." Ugh. "I'll see you there."

My fifty-ton blob of information-on-the-prince's-finances and I would be at the far-back table, fending off advances from my too-friendly boss, if Mom and Dad needed me.

I headed out to my truck.

Luckily, Dr. Shallenberger had agreed to meet me at the venue. I ran a heavy hand down my cheek as I drove. Referring to her as Kjersten when I was telling Mallory about my boss the other day had been a low blow—and disingenuous. On the fringes of a lie.

My soul was soot.

About a hundred cars lined the edges of the oval lawn when I pulled in. Mine was by far the least posh vehicle. I parked and headed up the grand portico between Doric columns and into the double doors.

"Calder!" Guess who ambushed me the second I set foot inside the warmth out of the cold. "You're here." My boss kissed me on each cheek, as if we were at cheek-kissing familiarity levels.

"Dr. Shallenberger." A chamber orchestra played instrumental Christmas pops somewhere, and she led me down steps into a marble-floored room. "Good evening."

"Don't you mean, Merry Christmas instead, darling?"

Darling!

"Besides. It's Kjersten tonight." She pronounced it *Share-ston*. "Let's not waste time. I'm dying for you to meet Dulcie. She's going to *like* you."

I'd met Dulcie. Dulcie had seen me with another woman. This … was just great.

I managed to keep her from taking my hand as we walked, but she did snag a flute of champagne off a waiter's tray, and downed it in one gulp. We passed a giant fireplace flanked by two towering, decorated Christmas trees. The whole place smelled like roast turkey and cranberry everything. New England loved its cranberries.

My eyes were peeled for Mallory. In a matter of seconds, I'd located her.

Oh, my giddy aunt. Mallory looked like a goddess tonight.

Her dark hair was piled high, exposing her neck's creamy-white skin. Just the perfect amount of blush graced her alabaster cheek. A white, strapless but long-sleeved gown covered her in something that sparkled—but those sparkles paled to the sparks flying off Mallory's smile and her whole being as she listened to whatever drippy thing Prince Reynard was telling her. Next, her infectious, distinctive laugh carried over top of all the other chatter in the room and hit my eardrum like a poison dart.

Reflex made me lift a hand to my ear to stop the pain.

"Calder, darling, this is Dulcie, my oldest and dearest friend."

Next thing I knew, I was getting the two-kiss treatment from another mid-forties woman who smelled of too much champagne all over again. I shook the hand of her stubby husband, whose shirt collar was two sizes too tight, making it seem like his head might pop off.

With a foggy look, Dulcie beamed at me, too inebriated to recall our previous meeting, it would seem. "My husband Charlton always says dating younger is good for your health and longevity, and Charlton is always right." Her speech had a slight slur.

Dating younger? Uh, they weren't referring to me and Share-ston, were they? "Dr. Shallenberger, I need to—"

I needed to get out of there. I needed to stop Mallory from making a colossal mistake—one worse than my mistake of withholding vital information from her that could affect her entire life.

"Oh, and Calder. Dulcie just told me she's also invited a former friend of yours. Once she heard you were my date tonight, she couldn't resist, she said. Who is the mystery guest? Do you know?" Dr. Shallenberger placed an unwelcome arm around my waist. "I'll let you speak with her if you promise not to forget whose dinner companion you are tonight."

"Speak to *her*?" As in, whom? I didn't know anyone in the area, and—

"Hi, Calder." A woman in a skintight, sequin-laden green dress undulated toward me, dark brown hair spilling over her shoulder. The hair wasn't her own, but the walk and the saccharine tones of her voice were ones I'd recognize anywhere.

"Alanis?" I croaked.

Chapter 20

Mallory

It was really happening. I was dressed like a princess, walking across the marble-floored ballroom of what felt like a royal palace on the arm of actual royalty. Tingles ran up and down my back, as if to signal that wishes had been granted. A real-live prince was looking at me like I was his dream come true. He kissed the back of my hand, and then each of my fingertips.

"You look ravishing, Mallory."

"You're not too bad yourself, Prince Reynard."

"Just call me Reynard." He looped my arm through his and we advanced into the room. From all sides, guests and Seacliff residents gave us nods of recognition, of approval, of envy. I'd never been looked at like this. It was amazing and terrifying at the same time. We stopped near the center of the ballroom, and I looked around for Calder.

No sign of him.

Instead of spending half an hour strategically arranging sparkle body powder in my décolletage, I should have used my time refreshing my memory on polite ways to address royalty by name. Your Majesty? Your Grace? I certainly wasn't going to call Prince Reynard's parents Joanna and Olav.

Worse, what was I supposed to say to them?

Reynard left my side and went to get us something from the punch bowl.

"Mallory? Is that you?" A woman's voice made me turn. "Mallory!" My college friend Beatrix threw her arms around me.

"It's so good to see you!" And I meant it. One ally in the room was so much better than zero. "What are you doing here?"

"Photographer for the event." She held up her camera. "It's something while I finish my book proposal."

We talked a bit about her book proposal, which was to be a historical account of the mansions in Seacliff if she could gain access to them, until Reynard returned, and it was time to go meet his parents.

First, though, I introduced Reynard to my friend. Beatrix took our photo. I'm sure I looked like a corpse—death by terror. Then, we left my one friend and went toward my dour introduction.

"Mother, Father." Reynard inclined his head. "This is Mallory, who has been restoring my castle. It's going to be better than"—he lowered his voice and let his eyes flit across the ballroom—"this one."

The queen followed his example, and her upper lip curled as if this place did *not* meet her expectations.

Wow. She must have very high standards, because Evergreen Point was gorgeous.

Luckily, for the next ten minutes, the king and queen chewed out Reynard in a foreign language that sounded like a mix of Finnish and Russian to my undeveloped ear.

I shifted my weight and tugged at my dress's sleeve-cuffs, wadding them into my fists. Should I cling to him? Look like we were a couple? What did he expect of me?

Come, meet my mother and father, he'd said. *This is Mallory,* he'd said.

And since then, I'd been the innocent bystander for what sounded a lot like a slaughter. Tone had to tell me all of it, since it happened in their native tongue.

"Mother and Father, I'm sure all your concerns over me will be allayed very soon. But we are being rude to my special guest." Reynard spoke in English during this final sally, for my benefit, it seemed.

Queen Joanna turned to me, finally acknowledging my awkward presence.

Instead of speaking any response, I just bowed my head.

Silence could be golden.

Well, one thing was for certain about King Olav and Queen Joanna: their looks directed at me could be described as *dour*. I'd give Reynard that. Imperious would be a close second though, particularly his mother's glares.

"This one is the good eater?" Queen Joanna said, looking across her formidable cheekbones' structure at me. "The one who makes the sounds?"

Oh, dear. The sounds. As of this moment, I wouldn't make a single sound—possibly ever again.

The king, now that he was appraising me, took a different attitude—more of a leer, as if he'd lick his chops any second.

Great.

Just marvelous.

"Hello, Prince Reynard." Into our little foursome, Rochelle poked her head. "Oh, and Mallory. You're with the prince. How nice. Prince Reynard, these must be your parents. They're very stylish, aren't they."

Everything about her was comfort. Folksy, relaxed comfort. Rochelle extended a hand to shake theirs. No nerdy curtsey, just friendship. After all, this was Rochelle's country, not theirs. And she should do the warm welcomes, not them.

Reynard's mother—Her Grace? Joanna? Queen … Something?— warmed slightly to Rochelle.

"Mother, this is the woman in charge of the entire crew who are remaking my home."

"A woman does that in this country." She sniffed. I said Joanna warmed, but that didn't mean she'd fully thawed. "What do the men do? Change diapers?"

To her immense credit, Rochelle didn't let the rudeness throw her for a single beat. In fact, she responded with her usually trilling laugh. "You bet they do, but they also run the crew. Darren"—she craned her neck as if looking for him—"I think he got dragged into the gravitational field of the hors d'oeuvres buffet—my food-fiend husband, does half the work, and I do the other half. Division of the labor in the career field. Same at home. In fact, when our son Calder was a baby, we took turns with diapers. I did days, and Darren did nights."

"Really." Queen Joanna looked away, as if for an escape route away from a conversation so ridiculous she couldn't bear another second of it. "The Americans are very evolved."

Rochelle pressed a hug around my shoulder. "You look so beautiful tonight, sweetie. I wish Calder could see you. He'd have the breath sucked right out of his lungs at your beauty."

"Thank you."

"She speaks!" King Olav said, followed by a guttural laugh. "You'll dine at my side, young Mallory Jameson."

"But the dinner cards have been placed by the hostess of the event," I *almost* said but stopped myself. Maybe it would be rude to contradict him, whether or not he was a king. He was an out-of-town guest. And the guest of honor, at that.

He should probably have things his way. He was probably very used to having things his way.

All the things, from the hungry-for-more-than-dinner look on his face.

"I'd be delighted."

"No, I'll be the delighted one. I hope you make the sounds."

Botheration. It was limestone, not marble, that opened up into sinkholes and swallowed people whole, right? And marble floors weren't the same as marble in nature.

All the same, I'd like to have disappeared.

"Calder!" A familiar name was shrieked at high volume somewhere across the room. My head automatically turned toward the voice.

A few feet away, near a pile of wrapped gifts, Calder stood with his back ramrod straight, while a stunning and statuesque brunette with the sexiest walk I would ever witness, stalked toward him in a green, sequined dress.

"Calder Kimball, as I live and breathe. I have been searching all over the world for you. And here you are, landing right beneath my feet, like the Christmas present I only whispered in Santa's ear to bring me." She threw her arms around his shoulders, pulling him close and breathing him in. "You don't know how much I've missed you these three years. Let's get back together."

Alanis!

Chapter 21

Calder

The perfume engulfed me, and with it, every memory swooped into my head as if they were all present at once: the day I met Alanis—*by accident*—at the gym in Boston; our first coffee shop date, and how she'd ordered the same drink as mine—also by accident—and the way I'd fallen for her ruse; our first kiss, in the moonlight near the St. Charles River; the drives in the country; the visits to historical sites around Boston, which she'd claimed to have haunted all her life; her dad's charming "Irish" accent; ring shopping; and then the big revelation of her trickery.

"Alanis. Or ... Trixie, was it?" Trixie's tricky lies, at my service.

"Shush, Calder. You know I'll always be your Alanis."

I stepped slightly backward, bumping into Dr. Shallenberger's drink. It splashed on my neck.

Instantly, Alanis had a handkerchief whipped from her clutch and was daubing at the spill. "There, that's better."

At some point in my life, I must have told someone or written somewhere that I admired old-fashioned things like women who carried a handkerchief. It was the kind of detail that Alanis had always honed in on, and probably still did.

"I'm so thankful Dulcie invited me," she said, slithering her arm to link it through mine, as if to pull me away from my boss's grasp. "I've been in the neighborhood ever so long."

"Ahem." Dr. Shallenberger pressed her foot down hard enough into my shoe it might make a crunching noise. "I don't believe we've been introduced."

Saved! Sort of.

And I was faced with a terrible choice: give ground to Dr. Shallenberger, or give ground to Alanis.

If I introduced my boss as my boss, Alanis won.

If I introduced her as *Kjersten, my date*, Dr. Shallenberger won.

Both ways, I was the loser.

Lose, lose, lose. I hated to lose.

And so, I did what my mom had accused me of a thousand times: I chickened out with a lame ploy. "Cough, c-cough, c-cough-cough." I made a fist and pressed it to my chest sideways. "Excuse me. I need a glass of water. Cough, cough, cough. Something's stuck."

Yeah, me. I was the stuck one. Like a pig.

Ducking slightly, I touched my forehead as if in apology and salute, and I made a dash for the door.

Alanis was at my side in an instant. "Calder. Thanks for figuring out a way we could be alone."

"I don't want to be alone with you." Or in a group. Or to ever see her again. "You're Socrates' hemlock to me."

"So you're saying I still have an effect."

Not a good one, hello. My fingers started shaking. I must have glanced down at them, because Alanis took them and pressed them to her collarbone.

"The *effect* seems to be a pure physical reaction. For me, too. Do you feel my pulsating heart? We always had that wild chemistry for each other. We should have worn a caution label—highly explosive."

She was the caution.

I was the idiot. The idiot with the blazing cheeks and the

117

jackrabbiting heart.

Why couldn't I just be calm and cool? I shouldn't react. I should be the coolest guy at this party, but seeing her brought back too much emotion.

I had to get out of this room, even though I might get fired for it.

I wrenched out of her grasp and jogged for the entryway.

"You're ditching me before dinner?" Dr. Shallenberger stalked toward me, talking the loud volume of the almost-drunk. "I trusted you, Calder, to be my arm candy for Dulcie's party. You were my golden ticket."

Ticket for what? She'd been drinking far too much and reading way too much Willy Wonka.

"Who's this woman?" Alanis turned on the charm. "You're dating again, Calder. I'd heard you were ready and waiting for me to come back."

"Heard from whom?" Oh, no. Not from Mom.

Dr. Shallenberger's gaze could have rivaled one of those cutting torch's beams as she sliced it across every inch of Alanis. "Come on, Calder. It's time for dinner."

"Calder, don't leave now. We've just seen each other again. You've been true to me all this time. Since our breakup, you haven't let anyone else in your heart, and neither have I. Your mom said I should give you another chance."

Mom and I would be having a serious talk.

A little growl escaped my boss, and her nails dug into my forearm.

"Oh, Alanis. You're here and looking just as lovely as ever." Speaking of Mom, Mom and Dad came up, warm as always, welcoming—and making a horrendous mess of everything. "I'm so glad you were able to come tonight. Three years is too long."

"Mom, Dad. This is Dr. Kjersten Shallenberger." Both names, plus the title. That worked. I had to pull their attention off Alanis. "She's at St. Dominic's with me. These are my parents, Rochelle and Darren Kimball."

The fingernail grip relaxed. Bless them for it, they absorbed Dr. Shallenberger's attention for the moment, so that I could think—and fast. Mom and Dad had obviously made the assumption that Alanis's presence was a good thing, a hopeful event—that she'd changed her mind about dumping me, or that their begging had worked magic.

Leave it to Alanis to exploit their misunderstanding.

I never should have let them think Alanis was the one who broke us up. Now, I'd put myself in this position.

"Oh, Calder, isn't it great that Alanis has spent the last couple of years on that humanitarian expedition to Central America and is still unattached?" Mom beamed.

Sure, she had. *Central America* probably meant the Midwest, maybe Chicago, and while there she'd been conning someone else.

Dr. Shallenberger had headed away, toward some people who'd waved her over, leaning on Dulcie's arm. Only Alanis and Mom and Dad remained nearby.

Alanis looked triumphant. "Your parents said isn't it great I'm back from Central America?"

"Yeah. Really great."

"It's good to be with you again, Calder." Alanis lowered her eyes. I'd seen that sexy look of hers in the past. It had worked on me so many times, muscle memory took over, and my hormones reacted to it—despite my head's silent scream of warning. "I want us to give things another chance."

She stepped nearer, and her scent enveloped me in a perfume I'd once thought the essence of divinity. Was I not over this woman? My head swirled. My brain turned to mush. Mom and Dad looked at me like I was finally the son they'd always wanted me to be.

"I promised your mom I'd help you come back to being part of the family. It's her greatest wish—and mine, too."

When she put it that way, the sand shifted beneath my feet. I'd never meant to drive a wedge between myself and my family by leaving to go teach. I'd wanted us to be united. I still wanted it, with all my heart. Mom and Dad were the greatest two living humans, and I wouldn't do anything to separate myself from them or their approval. If that meant being paired with Alanis, though …

"Come back and be part of the business, Calder. Let me stand at your side and strengthen you as you return to your rightful place."

Mom and Dad looked so hopeful, so anxious for me to say yes. This public place, with all the respectable people in their world milling around, was not the place for me to make a scene by telling them what a liar she'd been, or that I'd been the one who'd done the breaking up, not her.

Withholding information from key players in the drama of my life was coming back to bite me—big time tonight.

"Alanis, I think you have an idea where I stand." I squeezed her hand. "Since our last conversation, my opinion of you hasn't changed a bit."

"Then you'll have her back?" Mom asked eagerly. "Is my dream coming true?" She clapped her hands and bounced at little.

"Calder?" Mallory walked up. Something wasn't right. Her mascara was smudged, and her dress was a little askew.

My back straightened. "Mallory, are you all right?"

No, she wasn't. Her lower lip trembled. "I'm guessing this is Alanis."

"So, you've been talking about me to your employees. That's so sweet." Alanis attached herself to my arm like a barnacle. "Aren't you a cute little thing. Does she work for Royal Construction? How lucky for you, Mallory, getting to meet the heir to all the Kimball family owns. I bet you flirt with him all the time, but honey, his heart is taken." She placed a sensuous kiss below my ear.

Mallory's already distressed face distorted further. "Calder, what—?" She backed up a step, bumping into a waiter with a tray of champagne. The waiter barely salvaged the balance.

"Mallory—" I reached for her, but Alanis was faster.

Alanis reached out and grabbed Mallory's hand to shake it. "I'm

Calder's fiancée."

"Fiancée!" both Mallory and I said at once. I pulled my arm out of her grip. "Let's just slow down."

"Oh, I can take things slowly, that's fine. Your mom and I have a lot of wedding planning to do. Let's make it elaborate, maybe hold it at the Miro Mansion on the harbor, and we can invite everyone who's anyone."

Before I could pour ten buckets of water on that little flame—no matter how much it'd disappoint Mom and Dad—Mallory had fled, both emotionally and physically. Her white dress disappeared out a side door.

I yanked away from Alanis. "Now you've done it."

"Who is she? She's no one. I'm perfect for you. We're perfect together. Everyone can see it. Even you, if you'll just look for a split second."

Mom reached for me. "It's all we've prayed for." She gripped my hands as if for dear life. Dad rested a hand on my shoulder, one so heavy it could push me into the ground.

Six feet under.

Chapter 22

Mallory

His fiancée! But that woman was his nemesis. Wasn't it the Alanis he'd told me about, the woman who'd broken his heart?

I'd assumed he was attending the gala—he'd told me he had a date, but I thought it was with someone named Kjersten. He'd even walked in on the arm of some other woman, not Alanis.

Could it all have been a ruse to get himself back together with the woman who broke his heart?

Argh! I pulled at my hair. Tonight had been Dylan and the Independence Day dumping all over again. When would I ever learn? The second the guy's serious ex cracked open the door even a little to a reconciliation, he'd go racing back to her. Every time.

His parents had looked *elated.* They'd looked almost as exultant as Alanis herself. That woman had lorded it over me, too—as if she'd seen that I was competition and she wanted to bury me as fast as possible.

Worse, I'd just been insulted and ignored and scorned by Reynard's unpleasant royal parents. They'd looked at me like I was gum on the bottom of their shoes. At least his mother had. King Olav was too busy slobbering over me.

I tugged my coat more tightly against my chest as I walked toward my car. Prince Reynard had jettisoned himself off my radar screen in one hot second by introducing me to such a sleazy father. I definitely didn't want to run into the king in a castle stairway.

I spent time with Calder in a castle's stairway.

That'd never happen again.

For sure. Because I was quitting. This job had lost all its benefits for me. The construction people had my detailed designs. Rochelle and Calder could implement them. Oh, and Alanis could help! As Calder's fiancée, she would be around again all the time, just like Rochelle said a moment ago, exactly what she'd been praying for.

Rochelle. Praying for Alanis to return.

Be careful what you pray for.

I skittered over the wet pavement toward my car. At least I'd only agreed to meet Prince Reynard here and now wasn't forced to beg for a ride with him back to my bungalow.

Ride shares didn't really come to these parts—where every resident had multiple luxury vehicles, and most even had private helicopters.

"Wait, Mallory." A man's voice halted my steps.

I turned around. "Cald—" The second syllable died in my throat. "Oh, Reynard."

"Mallory." He panted. He was right in front of me, having covered the ground between us in three shakes. "I'm so sorry for my parents' behavior. It's inexcusable. I should have warned you more about them."

"You did mention they're dour." He'd left off the words *lecherous* and *condescending*.

"Yes, but they were beyond that. They were rude. They don't know how special you are."

He thought I was special? A little place inside me softened. "I'm not special."

"You most certainly are. And I mean to make them see it."

He was defending me? Well, that was new. But those people …

"I'm not sure. We don't really know each other very well." And the things I did know—I needed to think about more.

"But we have decades for that." He took my hands. "From the second I saw you, Mallory Jameson, I have been smitten by your beauty. But then, your charm eclipsed even that. Your honesty is incredibly refreshing. I am your slave."

He had a funny way of showing it. "You met me and then left for a few weeks. We shared exactly one conversation."

"I had some important things to attend to, so I could clear my life and make myself ready to be the right man for you."

What the—? "I'm ..." I couldn't think. I was mesmerized by his compliments and his assertions and his ... well, his royalty.

"You don't need to decide right now, of course." He took my hands in his, caressing the backs of mine with his thumb.

His hands were warm, soft. A little softer than I normally liked. I liked rough hands. Of course, he was a prince and wouldn't have had to do hard work that created calloused palms and fingers.

Royalty was what I'd wished for.

"Of course this is sudden. I couldn't speak sooner. But I intended to as soon as possible, and when you left before dinner, I couldn't let you get away without declaring myself."

He sounded just like one of those historical novels. It was everything I'd wished for in my little romantic teenage heart. My pulse pounded in my ears.

"I don't usually leave before dinner." I didn't *ever* leave before dinner. "I value dinner."

"I know you do." He smiled. It was smarmier tonight. Oily, or something. Then again, he was a prince. He was declaring himself to be interested in me, with a strong hint that he wanted to move things along quickly. "It's one of the things about you that captured my heart."

"One of?"

"That, and your dedication, and your creativity, and your knowledge of history, and your assertiveness when the time is correct for being assertive." He pulled me to him. "I could go on and on."

Could he, now? The little soft place for him grew—a lot.

He walked me to my car. "I won't pressure you for time." He pressed a kiss goodbye to the back of my hand.

Mercy.

"But maybe this will make you want to move more quickly."

Before I could react, he pounced! His mouth was on mine—a big, wet, smushy kiss. I pulled away from the unwelcome advance. "Hey, we're still getting to know each other."

"Good night, Mallory." He winked like he'd won the moment.

I got in my car, trembling. Tonight had been the worst—and the most confusing night of my life.

Calder was back with Alanis.

I had gotten my wish—a proposal from a prince.

So, why did I feel like I was making the worst mistake of my life?

Chapter 23

Calder

"Alanis!" I yanked myself out of her talons. "You are getting way ahead of yourself."

Mom stepped between us. "Son, when it's right, it's right. It's okay that the two of you hit the pause button on your relationship. But now, you can just pick up where you left off." She leaned closer and whispered, "I saw Mallory with the prince's family. They're taken with her, and we both know she's lucky to have been chosen by them."

"No, she isn't."

"You're sounding like sour grapes, son."

I couldn't do this with Mom. Not right then.

"I need to have a word with Alanis."

"Anything you have to say to me, you can say in front of Mom and Dad." Alanis had turned on her charm.

Dad was looking paternally at her, while he munched the food from the buffet. "Good to have you back, Alanis."

"No. It's not." If this was what the vixen wanted, a full airing, I wasn't going to deny her. "It's not good to have her back. The breakup wasn't Alanis's idea." Non-disclosure agreements be darned. "I dumped her when I discovered that she and her so-called father had targeted me in an elaborate fraud. Why you think you can come back here and dupe me again, I have no idea."

"You love me, Calder."

"I loved who you led me to believe you were." I turned to Mom and Dad. "This woman is a liar and a fake. She only wanted to con me into marrying her without a prenup, and then she and her partner would split the proceeds after the divorce."

"That can't be true." Mom took two steps backward, as if Alanis might be a plague carrier. "I should have seen through it."

Dad just gulped down his bite of barbecued chicken wing and shook his head. Disgust curled his upper lip.

"Right, Alanis?" I laser-stared her into the ground. "These are good people. Leave them alone."

"Calder, honey."

"Don't Calder-honey him." Dr. Shallenberger stomped up to my side. Her speech was slurred. "This guy is a great Hishhhtory teasher. Nobody defrauds teashers who work at St. Dominic's. He'sh a good boy. I love him, but he lovesh that Mallory person."

At which point, my boss—the mama bear—dropped to the ground.

As medics were called, Alanis put her tail between her legs and slunk out of the party.

"Good riddance," Mom said with a shudder. "I can't believe that happened."

Neither could I. None of it.

Instead, all I could think about was getting to, *that Mallory person.* Whether or not fortune had smiled on her by giving her the snowfall wish, I knew fortune had gotten it wrong.

I couldn't keep her in the dark any longer about Prince Reynard. Ignorance might be bliss, but it could be very dangerous, too.

"Mom and Dad, there's more I have to tell you, but I have to find Mallory."

"Yes, son. You do."

***

"Mallory!" I called when I got outside, running, but she was too far across the grass. For a second, she did look up—but that weasel-face Reynard stepped into her line of sight.

I skidded to a stop. I was too late. He was already right by her side, and she was soaking him up. I couldn't very well run up and call out, *He's got gambling debts and people hounding him for money!* I'd be acting like one of those people at weddings who speaks when asked to "speak now or forever hold their peace." They wait until that perilous moment, and it never ends well for the speaker, and the wedding always goes on.

"Mallory." Her name crossed my lips like a prayer. "Don't let him fool you."

But I was the bigger fool, standing stock-still, watching this horror play out.

Mallory was looking up at him skeptically, but then, I saw her visibly thaw.

And then—I nearly croaked! He yanked her into his arms and gave her the world's fastest but biggest kiss.

"No!" I shouted silently, but he sauntered off like he'd won the lottery, and Mallory got into her car and left.

Fool! I'd let her slip through my fingers. I'd allowed her to step into the unfinished conversation between Alanis and me and to totally get the wrong idea.

Now what should I do? Let Mallory fall for the attentions of the prince? Since the deal was sealed?

Mallory had always *wanted* a prince. She'd wished on the first snow for one as a girl, and now he'd come to her—in all his imperfections.

Well, who was I to judge? Was I the perfect guy?

Hardly. I'd spent the last three years—three *years*—hiding from a lie that I'd allowed the two greatest people in my life to believe. I'd changed professions. I'd denied my inheritance.

128

I was not the type of guy Mallory Jameson deserved.

She deserved someone truly royal—not just with the middle name Royal, or someone set to run a company with that word in the title.

The universe was kind. God did give people their deepest desires. I had seen it pan out right before my eyes, as she stood in her white dress in the moonlight filtered through the clouds.

She looked ethereal. Like the angel she was.

And he'd kissed her.

My hand balled into a fist. My eyes stung. And I'd lost her.

She was getting what she wanted: the richest man she could think of.

The idea soured in my mind. Curdling good feeling. Thinking deeper, Mallory wasn't different from every other woman. How had I been blind to it? Sure, she had her understandable reasons, considering her history. But did it matter what path had brought her to this point? She was opportunistic, just like every woman I'd ever let myself fall for.

I needed a stronger word for fool to apply to myself.

Chapter 24

Mallory

Back at the bungalow, I stumbled around, packing my things. I couldn't work on Reynard's project with Calder and his parents anymore, regardless of Reynard's wishes. I'd given my input. They'd finish implementing it.

I needed grounding. I needed the only family I had. And I needed to get out of there tonight—before Calder came back from the party, before the sight of him could make me change my mind and stay, try to win him away from that woman who'd been so terrible for him.

In all my life, since Mom died, I'd never been more confused or unsure of myself or my decisions. Calder was everything my heart needed. Prince Reynard was what … my stomach needed. Or was he? I really couldn't ever be in the same room with his disgusting dad again. But could we work around that?

I needed a place to land. I reached out to the only family I had.

"Emily? What are you doing Christmas Eve? Please say you're not working and that you need a couch surfer at your place. I'm not really up for pizza and endless YouTube videos at a cheap motel."

"Come on over." Emily was like a warm hug. "I'm going to be at work most of the week, but I'll be home on Christmas Eve after nine for

130

sure, and you're welcome to hang out day and night. If you want to bake, all the better."

Ah, the workaholic's Christmas. Well, it was better than being around no one at all.

Chapter 25

Calder

On the portico of the Delacourt mansion, I ran into Mom and Dad. I was shaking, after seeing that gut-wrenching sight, in addition to all the other crazy things that had happened over the past hour.

"There you are," Dad said.

"Hey," I managed. They descended the steps with me.

"Son!" Mom's jaw dropped so low that her chipped molar halfway back in her lower jaw showed. "You were not exaggerating when you described Alanis, I can tell. You gave us the honest truth."

"You know that I'm not usually one to lie deliberately. I sometimes withhold details if I am sure they will hurt those I love."

"I get that this deception was done in love for Dad and me, but why?" Mom paced the width of the hallway.

"I wanted to protect the reputation of Royal Construction."

"How so? At first, as I puzzled this out, I assumed you told us that Alanis dumped you so that we wouldn't think worse of her. That you didn't want us to know she was a bad person and get our feelings hurt."

"More like, I didn't want you to know how gullible I was. Alanis's name isn't even Alanis O'Houlihan. Her father isn't Irish. They're con artists. I didn't want you to know how close I'd come to tanking Royal Construction due to my bad judgment. If you didn't know, and if I left and went to work at St. Dominic's instead of with the family company, you'd be protected from future bad decisions I might make that would endanger everything your parents and you and Dad had built over the years."

Mom threw her arms around me. "Calder!" A huge sob rose up from her lungs. "I am so sorry—I only saw what I wanted to see."

Same here. "The O'Houlihans—who aren't even father and daughter, in truth—fooled us all. Don't feel bad."

"I mean about you. I love you, son. If you want to teach history, that's fine. But you have a heart of gold. And our company needs more hearts of gold. You're welcome anytime. We trust your judgment and love you and want you with us."

"I'll … I'll think about it." Meanwhile, Alanis had completed her destruction by wrecking my chances with Mallory, causing her to misunderstand and run headlong into the arms of the prince.

Mallory had been right about … well, about everything. I'd misjudged her motives, and applied the bad feelings I'd been harboring against Alanis. Mallory deserved the best. She deserved the happiness of receiving the dream she'd always wanted—in the way she'd always wanted.

Reynard couldn't give that to her.

But could I? My mind started cogitating a backdoor approach.

I worked on it during the drive back to Buckworth Castle. Sure enough, Mallory's car was already gone. My heart rent.

I'd probably seen her for the last time.

I went to my bungalow and curled in a ball on the bed. Every picture behind my closed eyes was of Mallory's beauty and grace, so I didn't shut them. I kept them open all night. They leaked a surprising amount, but by the next morning, I'd worked out some details and made some heart-choice decisions.

133

I could help her.

I loved Mallory enough to give her what she truly wanted. But to give it to her in full, I needed from my family—who I knew loved her, too.

Mom and Dad were in the pool room having breakfast. "Is something on your mind, son? Besides the obvious? I'm so sorry about Mallory. She left us a note."

I glanced at the note. Instead of letting out the primal paean cry from my heart, I sucked up my courage. "Mom, Dad. Do you think the corporation would negotiate a deal for my return?"

"You're coming back?" Mom's head whipped upward. "To work with us?"

"Yes, if you still want me. But I'll need to ask for an insane advance on my salary."

Chapter 26

Mallory

The first day at Emily's, I slept on her couch all day—the victim of a recurring dream that left me in a sweat every time I woke up. It went like this.

I slung my bag over my shoulder and exited the cottage at Buckworth Castle.

"Leaving?" Calder—could he have been loitering outside my door? "But the job is still a couple of weeks from being done."

"I spoke with your mom, and"—and Rochelle had understood. She'd been glad I was heading out, so I wouldn't be a distraction, keeping Calder from riveting his eyes on Rochelle's preferred choice of daughter-in-law—"and I think you all can carry on without me."

I pushed past him and headed for my car.

"Well, you'll be happy with your rich prince, I guess." He hadn't followed me but was just hurling the insult. "Rich guys finish first."

I turned around. "What—and the implication was that nice guys finish last?"

He obviously hadn't expected me to react. But his javelin had struck its mark, and it had pierced deep. How could I help but cry out?

Because yes. I was going for the rich guy. "Are you calling me a gold-digger?"

His voice grew dark. "If the shoe fits."

My toes curled involuntarily, and a reaction rose up from them to my chest and out my mouth. "Look, Calder. What's the difference between a woman wanting to marry someone who can take care of her and a man wanting to marry a beautiful woman? It's her prerogative to have standards about who she'll choose. It's the one decision in life in which we should be completely selfish—and being picky or discerning is utterly wise. Commendable, even!"

"Mallory, I—" The set of his jaw was hard.

My rant still had fuel. It bubbled over and flowed out in hot, red lava streams. "After marriage, it's time to become completely unselfish. Having kids helps develop that skill, but prior to, you have to seek your interests. It's the one and only choice in life that will determine our happiness. Or not. And I am determined to make the choice that will suit my needs—needs that life has taught me are important for my safety and security."

"You're choosing safety over freedom. Safety over love."

This last javelin struck its bullseye. I shrank from it. I wasn't making that choice!

I woke up from it for the third time, this time sweating and with heaving breaths.

I wasn't making that choice! Or was I?

Calder was taken. He and Alanis were back together—much to Darren and Rochelle's glee. Without Calder, I had no one. Whether or not the king and queen were great people like the Kimballs, I was otherwise alone. I was nearly thirty, and my prospects for an advantageous, poverty-proof marriage were dimming.

I needed Prince Reynard!

Besides, the prince was at my feet, begging for my attention. From what I could tell, he had many of the things my soul craved. Er, that I

136

had always told myself were important, at least.

I for sure *needed* the physical security he had to offer—even if his parents were jerks to me. We could live somewhere distant from the castle. We could be like Harry and Meghan and live in the United States. After all, Reynard had this property right here in Seacliff, and it was on its way to being perfect right now.

With Calder's help.

Ugh. If I were ever to live at Buckworth Castle with Reynard, I'd see Calder's touch everywhere I looked. The man who chose his rotten, no-good ex over me.

Fine. We'd have to find a different fixer-upper castle.

Another part of the dream came freight-training back to me.

"So, yeah, that's what I meant. Nice guys finish last."

"Honestly, Calder? I'm not sure I see a nice guy anywhere around." I squared my shoulders. *"Is a guy nice if he fills a woman's ears"*—and heart and head—*"with protests against his former girlfriend, and then agrees to marry her the second she resurfaces?"*

Resurfaces from her fiend pit?

"Marry her?" Calder's eyebrows flew upward. *"That's not ..."* Except he couldn't continue. Like I couldn't lie to him, he couldn't lie to me. *"You caught the wrong part of a conversation—one that I still need to clarify details of."*

"Telling someone to get lost because she's a liar who screwed up your life for three years isn't clarifying details, Calder." I huffed and turned to go. *"I really liked you, Calder. I was this close to falling in love with you."* But instead he'd chosen his own different fate. He was like that biblical dog who went back to its vomit. *"You get what you want in life, you know that?"*

I sprang away from the couch. I couldn't keep sleeping all day. I was creating nightmares for myself. As if my reality wasn't terrible enough—losing the first man I'd ever truly loved.

Wind blew outside the apartment, driving tiny, frozen snowflakes to pelt the windows of Emily's apartment.

If it'd been the first snow, I could have reached out my hand, caught some, and wished I'd never met Calder Kimball, the history-loving construction worker who'd stomped on my heart.

Chapter 27

Mallory

C hristmas in Boston is great. Even if you're alone most of the day, there are a lot of sights to see, amazing storefronts, roaming carolers in full Victorian costume on street corners with stovepipe hats upside down at their feet.

I plunked in a five-dollar bill.

Sure, I would like to have given more, but I mean, I was unemployed. I wanted to ask if they had room in their chorus for a short alto with no costume, and then I could split the tips.

Except I couldn't sing that well.

Emily texted. *I'm going to be home a lot later than I expected. Client nightmares.*

Emily was going to die of that corporate job. And I might die of boredom.

I walked through Copley Square, looking at the Beaux Arts Renaissance Revival features of the McKim Building at the Boston Public Library's cool architectural features along the way. Seeing beautiful design was great, but it wasn't the same as actually getting in and restoring something to its former beauty.

Or restoring it into a beautiful structure, like I'd been doing at

Buckworth Castle. Regardless of the people there and their quirks—and their rejection of me—the work had been really fulfilling. Beauty from ashes, all that.

Reynard texted me a photo of the latest progress on the castle. It was lovely. Perfect.

I attribute it all to you.

What could I respond to that compliment? Thank you? It seemed too accepting. I wasn't the one doing the work any longer. And I couldn't bring myself to mention Calder as being the one who was making the woodwork shine.

Calder took up way too much real estate in my brain.

My phone rang.

"Mallory Jameson?" It was the prince. He still didn't simply call me by my first name.

"Hello. How are you? Merry Christmas."

"Merry Christmas! I'm in my home country for the Christmas holiday. I had considered pressuring you into an answer and insisting you come for the family meal."

Ooh. Yikes. No more meals with them, please. "That's kind of you to think of me."

"As if I thought of anyone else."

"You're too kind." *Guilt. Guilt. Guilt*—stabbed in my eardrums. "Seriously," I said, and Calder's face danced before my eyes.

Of course, that meant I also heard his dream-accusation of my being a gold-digger.

Dream-Calder wasn't wrong. Which was what stung the most.

I just want to be sure I'll have food to eat! But then, another voice, my inner critic's, said, *Be honest. When was the last time you missed a meal involuntarily? Ten years ago?*

Ten. That was about right. I calculated. I'd been about nineteen, and my car had needed expensive repairs so that I could drive it for my third job, grocery delivery. The choice had been between a fixed car—and the subsequent income from work—and dinner for a week, even

140

ramen.

One week at age nineteen. Oh, and I'd been reading *Gone With the Wind* at the time—hence the Scarlett O'Hara fist-to-the-sky.

Humph. Scarlett had chosen the wrong guys, too.

Self-sabotaging, self-absorbed, self-destructing Scarlett. Was that how I was turning out?

Reynard went on, "Now, of course I would have invited you, but I know you need time to consider. I hope you are having a pleasant Christmastime."

"It's pleasant enough." I told him about Boston, about the frozen ponds where people ice skated en masse, about the carolers on the corner. "My old roommate is working too much, so it could be more festive and family-filled, but I'm watching some movies at night and stringing popcorn in the day." Between nightmares. "It's a holiday. Carpe diem."

"What is carpe diem? A new way to cook large fish?"

Stop. Don't tell me a European didn't know basic Latin! I gulped three times until Reynard filled the silence.

"None of that sounds like holiday fun. It all sounds like work. Why not go out to some clubs, dance and play cards?"

It was effort, sort of, but it was fun. "Do you work, Reynard?" I'd never asked him this before. "I guess being a prince of a nation is work." In a way. Did he make decisions, act as an ambassador of sorts? So many things I should have asked earlier! The list was endless!

"I ... have activities. They keep me occupied."

"Oh? Are they all in your homeland?" I needed to read up on his home's geography and all that. It was ridiculous—and telling—that I hadn't taken the time to do so.

"No, no. They're in various places." He made a weird sound that seemed to come from his throat. "Have you ever been to Monte Carlo?"

"Me?" Ha ha. Very funny. "You may not believe this, but I've been very few places in my life, and I've never left the Northeast."

The shock in his single-syllable laugh was palpable. "You must be joking! I must show you Monte Carlo! We will go for New Year's Eve. And then to Macao or Baccarat. And perhaps Las Vegas next. Have you never seen The Strip? The lights are impressive. Of course you've seen Atlantic City already, being a resident of America's East Coast."

"I mean, I've driven past it on the freeway, but I've never really had reason to stop there." It was a major gambling destination.

Come to think of it, so were all the other places he'd mentioned.

"You will love it. I will dress you in the most beautiful gowns and shoes and jewelry. You'll stand beside me and be—how do you say?—my Lady Luck?"

I liked the sound of this less and less. "You never really said whether you have a job."

The call dropped.

It often did with these trans-Atlantic calls he and I had shared half a dozen of over the past week. Before this one, however, I'd never been hung-up-on and felt so completely unsettled.

Truth dawned in a blinding ray: Reynard … was a gambler.

The last thing—very last, even after some kind of terrible disease—I needed in my life was a gambler.

I needed to get to the bottom of this. I dialed and dialed, but his phone went to voice mail every time I tried it over the next two days.

No luck.

Maybe *he* was having all the luck. Getting rich through the poker tables. My head throbbed.

Emily came home late on Christmas Eve night and found me on her couch, dialing him. She dragged in like she'd been run over by a UPS truck delivering last-minute Santa gifts.

"Whoa. Are you okay?" I brewed her a quick microwave cup of hot cocoa and brought it to where she looked dead on the couch. "What are they doing to you at that place, keeping you on a literal treadmill all day and half the night? It's Christmas Eve. You've got Ebenezer Scrooge as your overlord—*before* he met the three ghosts and had his heart melted by Tiny Tim."

"His name is Mr. Pokoa, not Scrooge. But I think he was trained in the same methods." Emily sipped her cocoa and let out a ragged sigh. "I'm sorry. I shouldn't have said yes about having you come for Christmas. I'm the worst holiday hostess of all time." Her eyes shut, and the mug looked like it would spill, so I took it from her hands.

"Hey, can you tell me," I said, still grappling with my Reynard doubts, "what Monte Carlo, Macao, Atlantic City, and Las Vegas all have in common?"

She opened one eye and used it to look at me dubiously. "Are you as naïve as you sound right now?" She harrumphed and sat up to drink more cocoa, taking the mug from the side table. "What's going on? Trouble in royal paradise?"

I took my own cup from the microwave and added the powdered packet of cocoa mix. The little marshmallows all collected on one side of the rim. "I really don't know." I should add a *him* to that sentence. "Don't worry. I'll figure it out."

"O, be wise. What can I say more?" Emily and her plethora of BrainyQuotes. "Have you even done your due diligence and looked up this prince online?"

Of course I had. I'd stalked him from the outset, but only for photos. Not to research his character. Probably a huge oversight.

I hedged, saying, "You know that's only going to net me stories of gossip. How can I use those as a source of information, when I have the chance to meet him in person and form my own opinions?"

The eyebrow arched.

Emily had done my due diligence for me, apparently.

"Don't tell me. I need to go for original sources. Like a good historian." A weird tickle started between my ear and jaw. I had to swallow twice to get it to go away. "Don't tell me. You know something about him. Just—forget it."

"Not even a one-line assessment?" She seemed to have one at the ready, and she might explode if she didn't get to share it.

"Fine. But only one line."

"It's actually a two-liner."

"You're killing me, Em." This was what made Emily a beast in the board room. She'd take your inch and turn it into a mile. "Okay. But then change the subject."

"Thanks. It's a good one. Let me find *Financial World*'s site." With a clear of her throat, she swiped through her phone, which appeared to have come out of its holster at quick-draw speed, and fired it at me. "Prince Reynard has achieved something extraordinary."

"I like the sound of that."

"Second line is the kicker, though." Emily read like she was delivering a speech. "Out of a truly crowded field, he has risen to the top and firmly wears the crown of Dumbest Royal in Europe."

My fingers went straight into my ears. "Stop. Just stop that." I knew for a fact he wasn't a mental midget, even if he obviously hadn't applied himself in his Latin classes. I'd been working around lecherous construction workers for years—a special breed of them whose vocabulary consisted only of four-letter words or indecent references. "He knows several languages, is quite articulate, and he's kind. Besides, an assessment of stupidity is usually applied by those who are jealous of those in power whose political views they disagree with."

There. I'd fired my rounds right back.

Apparently, they hit the mark because Emily backed down from Prince Reynard—and launched a different offensive. "Have you heard from Calder Royal?"

My cocoa burned my tongue. "I think you mean Calder Kimball."

"Don't tell me he's dropping his middle name and only going by his first and last these days."

"What are you talking about?" Tongue burning, I grabbed an ice cube and sucked on it, which gave me a speech impediment. "Hith name ithz Kimball."

Emily rolled her eyes at me. "Didn't you say your job is with Royal Construction?"

"Wathz." Past tense. I had quit the job—even before the project

144

was complete. I'd never done that before. It didn't sit well, but I knew when I wasn't wanted.

"Not the point."

"Look." I removed the ice cube. "I'm between jobs right now. What's your point? I was working for their subsidiary, with a couple named Rochelle and Darren Kimball. They were Calder's parents. The *Kimballs*. They do upscale renovations, but since it was their first true historical rehab project, I was brought in."

"Uh-huh." An imperious smirk worthy of Queen Joanna decorated her mouth. It wasn't nice.

"What. You're laughing at me. Or not. And it's making me feel stupid."

"Royal Construction is a multi-pronged conglomerate. It owns holdings in multiple construction-related businesses. It owns Terra Firma Concrete. It owns Statler Steel. It owns a hard-hat manufacturing company, a steel-toed boot making facility, a catering service solely serving construction sites, a crane manufacturer—oh, and they've recently diversified into a spin-off company where its owners spend all their discretionary work time, like during holidays. Guess who they are and what they do."

Oh, no. "Don't tell me. Renovation and rehab of historic houses." My hot cocoa sank somewhere lower than my stomach. "Rochelle and Darren own it? As in, they own all of it?"

"Her maiden name is Royal. She inherited the multi-million-dollar construction business her grandfather started fifty years ago, and she and her husband have turned it into some serious money."

Good grief. I set my cocoa on the coffee table and pushed it away from me. "A dynasty," I muttered.

"Their son, Calder Royal Kimball, was rumored to have stepped away from the business to pursue a different career, but according to recent business insider news, he may be returning to lead at least one of the subsidiary companies as he trains to take over the reins of the entire megalithic giant. You should know that Royal Construction is the biggest multi-faceted company on the East Coast. It eats every smaller company in its path and digests it into gold."

"That's a gross image." My cocoa curdled inside me.

"Sorry, but it's accurate."

I set down my mug and hugged my knees to my chest. "I know why it's happening. Calder is headed back to Royal Construction because his ex-girlfriend influenced him to do so." With Alanis at his side, his mom and dad were pleased as punch to have him back in their company and her back in his life—no matter how much she had hurt him and might hurt him again. I looked at Emily, my nose prickling. "He shouldn't go back to that woman."

"Men choose who they choose." She quirked her brow at me. "But I really think you had a shot." Her piteous look said, *Bummer, girl.*

Oh, anguish! I knew Calder well enough to know that if it would please his parents, he would endure a lot. He cared so much about protecting them and about their approval.

"Why do you look sick all of a sudden? You're not pregnant, are you?"

"Emily!" I could have chucked an ornament from the Christmas tree at her.

"Just kidding!" She reached over and patted my knee. "I know, you're smarting. But you do have a prince on the scene. Even if he's got problems, maybe being his ex will throw you into the path of other wealthy aristocrats. Your snowfall wish can still come true, right?"

"Prince Reynard isn't answering my calls."

She grimaced like neither of our snowfall wishes would ever come true.

However, right after I loaded our cocoa mugs into the dishwasher, my phone rang—Prince Reynard.

My heart stuttered. I answered, listened, and then said. "I'll watch for you. I can't believe you're here in Boston."

"Would it be Christmas without love?"

Good question.

146

We hung up.

"See?" Emily side-hugged me and grabbed an apple from the fridge. "I was right." She sniff-laughed, and I thought I heard her mutter *be careful what you wish for.* Then, she answered a phone call of her own, work-related, because she put on her game face.

"They're calling you for business? On Christmas Eve?" I put on my jacket and went down to meet Reynard, the man I'd wished into reality. The only man who seemed to want me.

Chapter 28

Mallory

I met Reynard outside Emily's apartment. Snow was falling, making the landscape white and clean and new.

"Mallory, my princess." Prince Reynard bowed to me, kissing the back of my hand like he had before. "It's a gift to see you."

All my life I'd wished to hear those words, and now I had heard them. Why didn't they settle right with me?

"It's such a surprise to see you." To say the least.

"When you described the beauties of Boston at Christmas, I could hardly stay away."

"But what about your family dinner?"

His face dropped. "My parents and I have had a disagreement." Then it brightened. "However, when I arrived here in Boston, I found that it had all been cleared up. They'll be pleased to see me when I return. Although, I must say it didn't quite work out the way I'd appreciate in *every* respect." The cloud returned.

I could read him like a farmer could read the weather. He was an open book—and something had happened. "Would you like to tell me about it?"

"Oh, no. I wouldn't trouble you with it for the world."

And he really didn't tell me.

Meanwhile, he continued walking along the red-brick path that took us along the famous Freedom Trail. We strolled through Boston Common, the beautiful public park, past the impressive fountain. Eventually we came to a magazine stand on the corner of Park and Tremont Streets, in front of the Park Street Church, and my stomach growled, just like it did anytime I saw a candy bar with peanuts in it. Peanuts had protein, and my body recognized it on sight.

"I'm famished. Could I stop for a quick minute?" I reached for my wallet.

Reynard mumbled an affirmative, but then—he started swatting at all the magazines, turning around the front copies on a few racks to face the covers backwards. "I'm so sorry you have to see this."

Um, they didn't carry inappropriate magazines at this stand—or at least they didn't put them out in front where any passerby could see.

"Calm down, my friend. It's not even swimsuit issue time of year." At Christmastime, everything had food on the cover. Or starlets in Santa hats showing off recipes.

He kept flipping them around.

I paid for my candy bar. Reynard might have if he hadn't been in such a weird panic. Calder had paid for everything when I was with him, even snacks from the register at the paint store.

I patted Reynard's shoulder, and it felt weird. It was the first time I'd touched him voluntarily. I dropped my hand. He and I weren't really progressing physically.

My last physical anything had been with Calder—and it'd been steam-powered.

Gah! I need to quit thinking about Calder. But how could I? He filled every crevice of my thoughts.

I wasn't being fair to Reynard.

Reynard's phone rang. I peeked at the screen and read the word *Mom.*

Weird. Nothing about Queen Joanna lent itself to being called

Mom. She was Mother if she merited any maternal appellation.

"Excuse me, Miss Jameson." He walked quickly down the sidewalk, leaving me to eat my Snickers in the shelter of the newsstand. I bought a second candy bar, a Payday like Calder had bought me in Anderson Lumber one day.

Lanny, the newsstand guy with the embroidered name on his jacket, reached over the counter and flipped the magazines back around, muttering something that decidedly refuted the Christmas Spirit.

The last one he flipped was *Financial World.* Ugh. That was the news site that hated Reynard, according to Emily's report of it. Maybe I should buy up all the copies and just throw them in the trash so that …

Wait a second.

Reynard's face was on the cover, and the headline read, *Royally Flushed: How a European Aristocrat Gambled Away His Family's—and His Nation's—Wealth.*

I picked it up.

"That's six bucks, lady." Lanny was tired of us both, apparently.

I paid and took the copy, shoving it inside my coat. It burned against my sweater, but I couldn't exactly be reading it when Reynard and I met up again. I started marching in the opposite direction. I wasn't ready to face him yet.

His words from earlier—that his problem had disappeared—rang back to me.

Something big had *definitely* happened.

And if the magazine's story was accurate, I definitely couldn't let this lie for long, but I wanted to give Reynard the chance to describe the situation before I absorbed the other side's version.

I'd easily know whether he was telling me the truth. That weather-vane expression of his—huh. I bet it would make him a terrible poker player.

Poker. Gambling. Lack of a poker-face. The two candy bars weren't settling well.

"You're all the way down the street!" Reynard wore the biggest, beamingest smile I'd seen him wear. "My mother sends you her love."

"Is that so?" I couldn't keep the doubt from my voice. "When I met her, she looked at me like I was three-day-old fish."

"No, no." Reynard was practically skipping as he took my arm and escorted me down the street. "She and Father were very angry with me that night, but all of that is fixed as of this morning, and they are nothing but smiles and sunshine for me. It feels like Christmas morning as a child."

I couldn't let it go on any longer. I stopped him near King's Chapel and pulled the magazine from my coat. "Let me venture a guess—it had something to do with this."

"Ah." His face fell. "You saw it, I guess." But the smile came back. "That was a nasty piece of writing, and they didn't get the numbers quite correct. They exaggerated by at least fifty million Euros."

I was a statue, just like gravestones in King's Chapel Burying Ground. Fifty million Euros! Those amounts were stratospheric!

"Stop, stop, bella. You look so worried."

"I am worried." Rightfully so. "You said the article is correct."

"Mostly, but I also said that the problem is solved."

"How?" I frowned, unable to formulate the word into a question. The guy was a gambler. A bad one. One that had ruined his family. Or almost had. I folded my arms over my chest. "Did you solve it? With more gambling?"

"No, no. That's all in the past." Gamblers often said that. Liars, too. "At least in the past until the restrictions are raised. Of course, I have you to thank for this rescue."

"Me!"

"Yes, you. A mysterious benefactor!"

"What do you mean?"

"Someone sent my creditors the balance of what I owed them—on one condition."

"What condition?" My fingers were tingling, and not from cold.

151

"It's so small, this condition. Merely that I not be allowed in their fine game-of-chance establishments for the period of five years after I marry."

Good condition. Then the other part hit me.

"Marry." A lump the size of Frosty the Snowman's head lodged in my throat. Around its bulk I managed, "Marry whom?"

Reynard laughed, his merriment echoing against the buildings around us. He threw his arms around me, lifted me, and swept me into a spin. "You, of course!"

Chapter 29

Mallory

Christmas Eve's church bells struck all over Boston, a call to evening Mass.

Though I'd never missed a Christmas Eve Mass, they called a different message to me. *Ask something else. Don't let this drop. But tell him no first.*

Although it was probably rude to leave a man in the King's Chapel Burying Ground when he'd more or less just proposed to me, in this case, cruel-to-be-kind principles came into play.

"I thank you for the honor of your attentions, Prince." Was there a yellow cab anywhere? I urgently needed to flee. "And I am happy for the kindness you've received. But you'd better go enjoy Christmas with your parents. You're right. Christmas isn't Christmas without love."

"You're not in love with me? But I'm standing right here." He looked around and then back at me.

Okay, maybe Emily's article about his intelligence hadn't been totally wrong, no matter how unkind.

"I'm sorry, but while reworking your home in Seacliff, I fell in love with someone else."

"Who?" He seemed so disbelieving, like how could a woman love any man other than him.

"You remember Calder."

"Of course. He was that worker man who followed you everywhere like a puppy." His upper lip curled. "But at the party, he was with the woman in green."

"I know." Boy, did I know it. "But it's unfair to you if I love him instead."

"You know what's funny? You don't hear that first name often, but he shares it with my benefactor."

Scrape me off the snowy sidewalk. "You're saying …" I gathered my million exploded cells back together long enough to ask, "Was your benefactor Calder Royal Kimball?"

"That's the one! I've never met him, so I was unsure how he would have known of my straits and been so generous." Oh, brother.

"Goodbye, Prince Reynard. I wish you the best." I blew him a kiss goodbye, and then I hailed a taxi and headed for Emily's apartment. "Stay out of the casinos."

"But, Mallory! I need to marry to keep the conditions."

"Reynard, you will do the right thing." Or so I hoped—for his sake. But he wouldn't be marrying me as part of it. "It'll make you a better husband to whomever you choose."

He looked crestfallen, but not devastated. He was a prince. He'd find his princess. Someone who liked dour people would be ideal.

My leg wouldn't stop bouncing. The cab driver kept eyeing me. I was a jittery mess, probably looked like a drug addict. Why had Calder paid off Reynard's debts? Especially when he was with Alanis, now? And with what money? Could it have been out of guilt for ditching me so cruelly?

I ran up the steps to Emily's apartment. She wasn't there, but I gathered my things. I had to do something, but what? Could I go to Seacliff? It seemed strange to barge in on someone's Christmas Eve dinner uninvited, and possibly unwanted. But I needed to see him, thank him, and to find out the truth.

And I needed to *tell him* the truth. That I was in love with him, that I'd been wrong to chase Prince Reynard, to ignore signs of the prince's bad character, that I'd been a fool not to see Calder's greatness when he was right in front of me.

The bedroom door banged open, and Emily stood there. "What's going on?"

My bag was packed, and I went in the bathroom to grab my shampoo and toothbrush. "I'm not sure, but I think I'm driving to Rhode Island right now."

"Now? But … what about Prince Smartypants? Why aren't you with him?"

I plopped the magazine in her lap. "Look at this."

She fanned the pages with her thumb and handed it back to me. "Yeah, that's the article I was referring to when I read you that mean line."

"Emily." I frowned. "It's still a really mean headline, whether I'm marrying him or not." I told her about the proposal and my exit at King's Chapel Burying Ground.

"Seems fitting. The death should be at a burying ground."

"Death!"

"Of his hopes to marry you. Now, look at the title of the magazine, girl. *Financial World.* You didn't let me share more lines, or you would have seen that he's known as the dumbest royal alive *when it comes to money.*"

Oh, that. Fine, I'd concede that point. "Well, he's out of trouble, as long as he finds someone else to marry."

Her eyes popped open. "How?"

I told her. She took a deep breath and let it out slowly. "Calder Royal is in love with you."

"He's with his ex-girlfriend."

"Not according to the news I saw. They were dubbing him an eligible bachelor."

"She said he was her fiancé. I heard it from her own over-

155

lipsticked lips." And I'd curdled like lemon juice and milk. "I'm only going to Seacliff to thank him and to find out what his motivation was for bailing out Reynard." *Could his motivation be love for me? A consolation prize for not loving me enough to stave off Alanis?* "It's a big enough deal I should thank him in person. And, you know, apologize."

I really needed to apologize. Because of those nightmares, I'd convinced myself Calder thought of me as nothing but a gold-digger, and I couldn't stand to have him be out there in the world thinking badly of me.

"Apologizing is good." Emily bit her lower lip. "Forgiveness—when we're asking it, we definitely want to receive it, so we should give it just as freely."

If she was hinting at something besides Calder, and she definitely seemed to be, I wasn't following. "Are you talking about something or someone in particular?"

She aimed a look at me. "Your parents, maybe?"

"They're gone. Or dead."

"And?"

"And they wouldn't know or care if I forgave them at this point."

"Maybe not, but you would."

Oh.

Yeah.

The idea settled over me like a heavy mist.

"It's time, Mallory. You need to allow them to have been human and to have made awful mistakes. Just like everyone else."

I pressed the spot between my brows and rubbed it as if it would make the truth sink in faster. Emily was right, and I knew it. "I'll work on it." It'd take time. "I really will."

"That's good. I'll bet Calder can forgive you, too."

Calder. *Calder!* "Emily, it's awful. I should have chosen him—based on his merits, not on his bank account. If I'd just responded to Calder's interest in me sooner and better, he wouldn't have been tempted to get back together with Alanis. I knew he was into me, but I couldn't see him because my mistaken interest in Prince Reynard eclipsed the truth. I'm in love with him."

There. I'd admitted it aloud to Emily, now, too. And to myself for the second time. I was in love with Calder Kimball.

Emily lifted a weak fist of victory. "Yay for true love." But then she made me sit next to her and share the throw blanket across her lap. "Tell me this thing, though. Why do you want a rich man these days, anyway?"

We'd been over this. "Same reasons as always."

"But ..." Emily reached behind a throw pillow and grabbed her laptop. A moment later, she opened a site with a bunch of numbers on it.

Emily did love crunching the numbers.

"What's this?"

"Your investment portfolio? I'm guessing since you don't recognize it, you haven't been watching the balance change."

"Oh, that." The letters came to me monthly about it. I never opened them. They'd probably have the original thousand dollars I'd handed over to Emily when I'd asked her to be my investment counselor a few years ago—but with a shrunken balance each time, just like my bank balance between jobs. "Do I have to? It's late. It's Christmas Eve." Most of all, I wanted to get on the road to find Calder, but in spite of that I said, "Let's just sing some carols and eat ourselves sick on chocolate. It's the American dream."

"No, this is the American dream." She aimed the screen at me and touched a large number.

"What—I think you mean that's *your* account's balance, not mine."

"Mallory." Emily slapped the lid of her laptop shut. "You've been funneling me capital every month for years. Do you think I, your former roommate and best friend forever and ever, would do anything irresponsible with that trust?"

"Um, no?" The truth prickled at my skin, but it took a while to pierce its way through to my understanding. "You mean, you took my monthly pittance and turned it into"—I waved at the closed laptop—"that much money?" My brain did some quick calculations. "That is … a *lot* of months of groceries."

With lips mashed into a smug line, she nodded at me, her eyes squinched shut.

"That's enough that I could shop in the *nice* supermarket."

"For the rest of your life."

"Emily." I gulped. Twice. "How did you do that?"

"That's what my firm does. They take people's money, risk it, and garner rewards."

"Great rewards." Good night! My adrenaline buzzed, and I got up and paced the room at a rate where the carpet could wear out in minutes.

"So, you're saying … I don't need to marry a rich guy to keep myself from going hungry?"

"Do you even check your bank account balance, honey?"

"I just saw it." I staggered.

"No, that was your investment portfolio. I'm talking about your checking and savings balances."

"What?"

"Hello there. They're in the very comfortable range as well. You could buy property with them. Real estate. Maybe even that dorky-looking castle you were renovating."

Very comfortable. In Emily's terms, that must mean it was huge. She dealt with the biggest clients ever.

"I don't look, but I also never spend. I just sock it all away into savings." With a nudge from Emily, I opened my app and looked at my bank statement. "What? Seriously?"

"I made sure you had an interest-bearing account, remember?" She scratched her forehead and yawned. "It was an H-fund, the most aggressive risk level for that bank of yours, and they've had an excellent year."

Oh, my goodness. She'd put my money in a high-risk fund, and I hadn't paid attention? I should have, but I merely trusted her. And boy-howdy, what a payoff for that trust! Between my portfolio and my savings account, I was … not poor anymore! It'd take me decades to spend this much on rent or groceries or transportation.

I could … go to Greece and Italy!

"Thank you, Emily. Thank you so much!" I threw my arms around her neck. "But I'll still eat macaroni and cheese from a box, I promise."

"I know you will, sweetie. And this isn't all me. You're the one who earned the money and had the discipline to save it and the courage to let it be invested."

Whoa. I got up and paced some more. She curled up into a ball. "No carols and chocolate feast for me tonight. You go do what you're doing. Tell Calder Kimball, the hot construction worker hi from me."

"I will." Wherever he was.

Where was he on Christmas Eve? I thought about calling him. I couldn't make any good decisions—not in this jumbled, elated state of mind. I'd just have to go back to Seacliff. Bag over my shoulder, I opened the door to the outside and stepped onto the stoop.

It wasn't the first snow of the season, but I needed this anyway. I caught a snowflake on my palm—the first one I saw.

Eyes closed, I wished—hard—for the thing my heart needed most.

Chapter 30

Calder

"No, Mom. It's late. I'm out of town. I'm not going to be there tonight at all. Maybe I can go to church with you tomorrow, but that's it." I was talking too loudly into the phone—on the street—in a town where I'd rarely been before. "I just have … something to do."

Someone to try to catch a glimpse of, more like.

If I can see her just one more time, then I can let her go.

"Bye, Mom. I'll be there eventually. I promise."

A cold, wet prickle stung my cheek. Snow? I whipped off my glove and held my palm open.

Wishing was stupid, but who cared? Wishes sometimes happened, and Mallory had wished on love. My current wish was a little low—in that it would more or less cancel out Mallory's childhood wish—but wishes were wishes. Pure and simple.

A flake landed in my hand! I closed my fingers around it … and *wished*.

A few blocks later, I arrived at the address Reynard had given me. *More like, I'd squeezed out of him as part of the stipulations.* It wasn't that I had stalker tendencies—I just wanted one last glimpse before

Mallory left my life forever to go off with Reynard the Royal and become a bona fide princess.

My study of the accession laws of the guy's homeland hadn't turned up information as to Mallory's likelihood of becoming part of the ruling decision-making for their country, but they'd be wise if the royal family heeded any counsel she chose to give them. She was the brightest, wisest, most determined woman I'd ever met.

I was in love with her.

But since I couldn't have her, she deserved to marry a guy who had a clean slate, at least to start out with.

What choice did I have but to give her that?

It was a Christmas gift. An engagement present. It made a serious dent in my net worth, but Mallory was worth it.

A single light was on in the windows of the apartment where she was supposedly staying. After fifteen minutes, though, no one had looked out the curtains.

Not that they should! What was I thinking?

Setting down the pebbles I'd intended to throw at the window, and picking up the pieces of my stalker dignity, I climbed the steps and pressed the intercom for apartment nine. "Merry Christmas?" I ventured, clearing my throat too many times. "I'm looking for Mallory Jameson."

A loud yawn followed. "Mallory?" Another yawn. "Sorry, but you just missed her. She's gone out of town."

A groan roiled up from the depths of my soul. "Did she go with Reynard?"

"Who is this? I don't answer reporters' questions. I'm hanging up now."

"No! Wait, no! This is Calder, Mallory's friend."

A long silence. I'd lost her. Should I ring again? I backed up, hope draining from me. "Well, thanks anyway."

"You mean *the* Calder?" The roommate was still there on the intercom! "Calder Royal Kimball?"

"That's me." Calder Royal Kimball, as I was about to become known once again. "Is this her friend Emily?"

"Uh-huh. Calder, she's heading to Seacliff, Rhode Island."

***

The snow dissipated as I roared southward. A full moon peered through the clouds, and then it dominated a clear night sky.

Eighty-two minutes and barely avoiding three speeding tickets later, my truck's tires spewed gravel on the circular drive of Buckworth Castle. It looked nothing like it had when we started. All the medieval stone façades were gone, and only the original design remained.

The building was pretty in the moonlight, as the clouds had cleared up. The additional landscaping lights aimed at the renewed blush-colored paint on the stucco. A blush just the color of Mallory's porcelain bisque cheek when I'd first kissed her.

I parked, tore across the drive, and burst into the pool house. "Mom?" I was shouting, and I didn't care.

There, Mom and Dad and Mallory were lounging together on the edge of the pool, plates of Christmas Eve dinner in their hands and their feet dangling in the heated water.

"It's ten p.m. You're eating dinner?"

"Calder! You're here!" Mom jumped up, taking her plate and dragging Dad to his feet as well. "Ten is when our company arrived. You eat when hungry people appear. Don't you have good timing? Dad and I will go fix you a plate. Our chef has the night off, so Dad and I will be in the kitchen. For a *long* time, very long, preparing your plate of food. You just relax and talk to Mallory." She leaned in close to me. "And don't worry—I already did the sackcloth and ashes apology for pushing Alanis on you. She was very understanding."

Mom and Dad left, not bothering to hide their glee. At least they'd given us privacy.

My gaze riveted on Mallory. She set her plate at her side and moved to stand beside the pool. A roaring fire blazed in the hearth.

I raced to her side to help her up. "What are you doing here? I

162

thought you'd be on a private jet to hang out with dour King Olav and Queen Joanna and their dour servants."

She smiled, and my power of speech disintegrated. Her smile was lethal to complex thought.

"Your mom said the remodel is nearly done inside and that you might like to take me on a tour of the interior and the grounds."

Uh-huh. Mallory took my hand. I soared—just floated beside her as she led me across the expanse between the pool house and the main mansion.

This wasn't real. There'd been a car accident. I'd rolled my truck in the snow outside Boston, and now I was having one of those out-of-body Dickensian experiences, starring Mallory as *The Ghost of Christmas That Might Have Been.*

"Oh, wow!" She pressed on the light when we went into the main living area where I'd first laid eyes on her. "The switch plate is exactly period correct." She pressed the bottom button, and the top one popped out, and vice versa. "I feel like I've stepped into a time machine a hundred years ago."

"We took all your notes and implemented them."

"Where did you even find this wallpaper?" She sounded giddy with joy. "It's amazing."

I took her through the rest of the main floor of Buckworth Castle, showing her everything—and she focused on all the right details and delighted at all the right places—the things we'd taken so many pains to get right.

We went up and up, through the first floor, the second floor, and we ended by climbing the stairs to the cupola. The parquet floor decorated the edges of the octagonal room. A beautiful rug filled the center of the floor. Through all eight windows, the moonlight streamed, and it lit the sea beyond the cliff. Breaking waves crashed in regular, heart-beat-like rhythm on the rocks.

My own heartbeat was nearly as loud as the massive ocean, though. I was within touching distance of Mallory—and she was with me, not Reynard. But why?

Normalcy of thought patterns came and went—being plagued by spikes of elation and disbelief, as well as pure, primal longing to take her in my arms.

"I'm so impressed, Calder." She turned to me and looked up at me with her dark, beautiful eyes. "You have made this mess into a respectable castle. Fit for any royal."

My biggest question splashed forth like the Krakatoa tidal wave of the 1880s. "Mallory, why aren't you with Reynard?"

"I suspect it's the same reason you're not with Alanis. Or with that other woman—your boss?"

"Oh." I let the implications sink over me. "And is it correlated to the reason I'm with you?" I caught her gaze in my own. I was not letting it go any more than a vise would let go of a board it was clamping. "Because I'm in love with you and would do anything—even drive much too fast on winding, snowy roads—to be with you?"

"Correlated, I believe so." A slow smile spread across her pretty face.

"Mallory, you're who I wished for on the first snowfall in Boston tonight."

"You were in Boston? You drove all the way there and all the way back? And you wished for *me*?"

"Mm-hmm. How could I wish otherwise? You're my morning and evening star. My Venus, my Athena."

"Calder, I bet your history classes are amazing. You have all of the ancient past at your beck and call. Including Latin."

"I think you mean Pig Latin." I stepped closer to her, taking her in my arms. She smelled like Christmas and fresh starts. "But you should know, I've decided not to go back to teaching." I pulled her closer.

"Is that so?" She ran her hand up my chest and sent it around the back of my neck, where she caressed my skin and demolished my thoughts. "I'm sure your boss will miss you."

"My boss found someone else to teach history." After the house party at Evergreen Point, actually. Someone more amenable to her advances. "St. Dominic's knows I'm replaceable there."

"But not in other places." Her other hand had come upward and was twirling a strand of my hair.

"No. Not everywhere."

"Not in my life."

That was the opening I needed. I bent my head, pulled her tight to me, and pressed a kiss to her supple mouth like her touch was oxygen.

Mallory returned my kiss with a power I'd never experienced. The kiss we created tore me in pieces and then put me back together in a wholly revised picture of myself—one where I was a new creature with strength and purpose and direction.

"I'm in love with you, Mallory Jameson."

"I know."

"How did you figure it out?" I asked between repetitions of our rapture.

"Calder—what you did for the prince—" She kissed me again, but then pulled away. "Was it for the prince?"

She should understand it all. "I did it for you. Not him, make no mistake. I wanted you to have the financial security you always wished for. I knew he couldn't provide it and that"—something caught in my throat, a hitch—"you deserved it."

She kissed me again, like we were in the waves that roared below, rising and falling, surging and receding, a churning of the eternal.

"Don't worry, though," she said, taking a breath. "I'm not worrying about those things anymore. I've gotten all that straightened around in my life."

Oh, she had? "Can I ask how?"

She explained her unexpected investment portfolio.

"That friend of yours is a skilled investor."

"Calder. You knew early on about Prince Reynard's troubles." I took her and we sat on one of the eight window seats in the cupola's geometry. "You must have had a depth of knowledge by the time you orchestrated his bail-out this week. He told me a few of the particulars." She described them, but Reynard had only skimmed the surface of what I'd required of him in return. "Why didn't you tell me when you first found out?"

"Because, as you told me, he was your wish come true." I pressed my hand over hers.

"No, that's you." Mallory placed her head on my shoulder, and said with a sweet sigh, "I love you, Calder. I did from the first minutes we met—which was what scared me."

"Me? Scary? I'm a history teacher. The least intimidating creature on earth."

"You weren't what I was expecting. I should have looked closer—I should have opened my eyes sooner."

"I should have opened my mouth sooner."

"Well, put that mouth to good use now, please."

Another kiss, and another, filled the windows of the bright Christmas night with the glow of love. I loved this woman. We had all things bright and beautiful before us, here, in this seaside castle. Together—the past, present, and future. All time bound together by love.

As we descended the winding staircase, onto the landing, and then down the grand staircase, Mallory ran a hand down the high-gloss mahogany banister. "I'm going to miss this place so much."

"Oh? Why?"

A half-laugh. "Are you just being silly? Because it's where I fell in love with you. It's where I first kissed you. It's sacred ground."

"Then I have something important to tell you."

"You do?" She stopped. "I'm ready for good news."

"As part of the agreement between Reynard and me, he signed over the deed of Buckworth Castle."

"To you?"

"To me. And my heirs."

"You have heirs?"

"I hope to. Soon."

Her brow raised. "How soon?"

"Very soon."

Epilogue

Emily

"Thank you so much for being here." Glowing bride Mallory hugged me, looking like a princess. "I couldn't have asked for more helpful bridesmaids."

"You'd better get on your way." Jayne straightened Mallory's veil. "We'll be waiting near the preacher for you."

"I can't believe this is happening. Calder is a total prince." Mallory squeezed both our hands, and then scurried off to where Calder's dad was waiting to walk her down the aisle. Pretty sweet setup, I thought.

Jayne and I went to take our places.

"Mallory isn't wrong about Calder being a prince." Jayne and I picked our way over the grassy area to our spots overlooking the ocean. The waves roared serenely, as if they had awaited this day for eons. "When I found out they were engaged, it seemed a hundred percent perfect."

So strange that Jayne had met Calder first—and that she'd thought him a perfect match for Mallory. Which he was.

"Small world." Really small. Strains of a string quartet floated on the breeze, playing something that, Mallory said, was au courant a century ago at the time their mansion was built. "I don't think they had any choice but to make their wedding historically accurate to the venue's time-period." I leaned my head on Jayne's shoulder, a little emotional in the moment. "Her dress is Gilded Age perfection."

"She always did look best in white." Jayne waved her mini-bouquet of flowers. "It's so beautiful, what they did to restore the mansion. I love that they changed the name back to its original title, too. And wow. I love this view, too. Do you think I could do an on-location segment of my morning show out here, or would the waves be too much background noise?"

Jayne went on about her plans to highlight Seacliff Chateau on her and her husband's television program, and to showcase the interior design in six months at Christmas again.

"I, for one, think you should come down to stay here every chance you get," she said. Of course, she'd made her first snowfall wish come true at a vacation home, so she probably thought that would work for everyone. "It's not that far from Boston."

"It might as well be a million years away." Besides, there were no bridges in Seacliff, Rhode Island, and I'd wished for a bridge kiss and proposal. "I'm resigning myself to being married to my work."

The quartet would play the Wedding March soon, and we'd have to quit talking. I'd be fine with that. I didn't want to think about my failure in love. Yes, I was dating a guy at work, but it was new, and he was as nose-to-the-grindstone as I was. We might never come up for relationship air long enough to breathe life into our love.

But it wasn't impossible. Justin was pretty great.

Oh, but I want my snowfall wish to come true like theirs. Jayne was married to a guy who just got a job as an English teacher—her wish. Mallory was fifteen minutes from I do with a man so noble he deserved a crown.

Then there was me.

No kiss on a bridge, let alone a proposal, on my horizon.

But if their wishes had come true, couldn't mine?

169

Snowfall Wishes Series

Wildwood Lodge

Seacliff Chateau

Maplebrook Bridge

Acknowledgments

Thanks go to the wonderful staff at the Eastern Arizona College Library for their incredible support and accommodation while this book was created.

Many thanks to CJ Anaya, Mary Mintz, and Paula Bothwell, without whose help this book wouldn't have come into being.

More thanks to Suzy, Dacia, Debbie, and Jeanie for giving early encouragement.

Also, huge gratitude to Shaela at Blue Water Books for her gorgeous covers. You have a wonderful talent and a beautiful soul.

Finally, never-ending thanks to my husband, who is my "alpha reader" and first in everything in my heart.

About the Author

Jennifer Griffith is the *USA Today* bestselling author of clean, escapist fiction she calls Cotton Candy for the Soul. She and her family live in the rural Arizona desert, where the winter is seldom snowy, but she loves Christmas and cocoa and all things cozy.

Made in the USA
Columbia, SC
09 February 2022